# The Aloha Murders

## By

## Manya Nogg

Copyright © 2018 Manya Nogg
All rights reserved.
AEL PUBLISHING
a division of Actors Etc. Limited
Omaha, Nebraska

ISBN-13: 978-0-9966740-3-4


Sherry Fletcher - Editor
Brian F. Nicol - Editorial consultant
L. R. Nogg – Cover photo and design

## Other books by Manya Nogg

**AGE IS JUST A NUMBER AND MINE IS UNLISTED**
A Memoir That Spotlights Sixty Years in Show Business

**A SHADOW IN VENICE**

# The Aloha Murders

# Prologue

It was night in the Nu-uan Valley outside Honolulu. The moonlight dusted the ridgeback folds of the mountainside. Far below, a boy, clad only in pajamas, wandered through a vine-encrusted rain forest. His bare feet padded through the underbrush while the noisy chatter of night insects filled the warm, caressing wind.

The gentle breeze died, and all sound stopped. The boy felt a tremor beneath his feet which stopped his forward movement. A steady rumbling grew louder, then a drum, accompanied by a flute's high-pitched cry, stabbed the air.

The boy crouched down, whimpering, and watched the ghostly vision of a feathered cape brush past. Hawaiian chanting replaced the cry of the flute. A word escaped the boy's lips: hauka'i-po – the night marchers!

Moments later, the breeze returned, bringing back the night sounds. One word lingered in the night and echoed around the boy. Revenge … *Revenge … Revenge!*

---

The dreamer awoke with a start, sweat soaking the bedclothes. Not that nightmare again! It had been visiting regularly for more than 40 years. When would it end? To calm jangled nerves, the dreamer settled down with the newspaper.

"Hmm, there's a sovereignty rally tonight on the Palace grounds. As a Hawaiian member of the movement, he'll be there wearing his cape. What a lovely time for him to meet his maker."

# Chapter 1

The killer screamed in frustration at the television news. A nobody had been killed at Iolani Palace last night. The gun must strike again.

---

The secretary in the office of Kaiawoaho Church replaced the receiver, then stood staring down at the phone with a puzzled look on her face. A fellow worker came into the room and asked her what the matter was.

"That was a very strange phone call. The person wanted to know if we have any activities going on at the church tonight, especially something with music."

"Why did they want to know that?"

"I got the impression it was a tourist. They're always calling about coming in at odd hours. Anyway, I told him, or her, that we do have a wedding scheduled for 8 p.m."

"What do you mean him or her?"

"The caller's voice was garbled, like laryngitis or something. Whoever it was didn't sound like they were in any shape to be on the street tonight."

---

The office supply store clerk distractedly observed the many customers testing the latest in typewriters. One customer seemed to be typing something real — a letter, perhaps. The clerk rubbed his head in an effort to clear the noise and turned his back to answer the telephone. When he hung up and hurried over to the typewriter, the customer had vanished.

# Chapter 2

Kamuela Winslow stood chain-smoking in the glow of a street lamp outside the closed Mission Houses Museum. He lifted the note to read it again.

"Meet me in the back garden of the Mission Houses tonight at 8:10. You'll learn something profitable," the note read. He crumpled it and added it to the pile of cigarette butts under the lamp.

Suddenly, he heard a sound over the music coming from the church across the street. "Hello! Hello, who's there?" he called.

An apparition emerged from the shadows wearing a long dress. An outstretched hand fired the gun it was holding.

The killer spoke in a hoarse whisper, "I didn't make a mistake *this* time. I'll dispose of this dress and the gun and there will be no loose ends."

# Chapter 3

The officer at the security check point hesitated, then allowed the dirt-stained slob to enter Honolulu's police headquarters. The man was exhausted and moved slowly down the hall to the bank of elevators. Entering one, he pushed a button, then leaned against the wall for support. His blonde hair was dirty and disheveled. A three-day growth of beard shadowed his jaw. Dark circles formed a stain under his eyes.

He couldn't remember the last time he felt this tired. He was a seasoned warrior with enormous stamina, but Hawaii got to him. Or maybe it was a combination of leaving the mainland in a hurry, with a lot of unresolved problems, and the frustration of the wild goose chase he'd been on since his arrival in Honolulu.

He checked the listings on the wall sign, then dragged himself off the elevator in the direction that pointed to "Homicide."

Lieutenant Kaloke "Cholly" Chan, a beautiful, Hawaiian-Asian woman, sipped at the lousy station-house brew as she paced in front of Captain Kimo Kahana's desk. Her boss tried to ignore the movement as he signed some reports, but finally blurted out, "Park your okole in a chair before you wear out my rug." The Captain could see that she was pissed off at him and was concerned that she'd take it out on the new partner she would soon be meeting.

She gave him a look that would freeze-dry coffee, then plopped into one of the leather chairs in front of his desk. A few drops of coffee sloshed out of the cup and onto the crease of her uniform pants. Cholly dabbed them away with a tissue from the desk. For the umpteenth time, she glanced at her watch. She didn't want this new partner, and to make matters worse, punctuality wasn't his strong suit. She snapped at the Captain, "I've got to get back to work! With Kam's accident, I need …."

Cholly's long-time partner, Kam Alpa, had been injured two weeks earlier and since then Captain Kahana had kept Cholly in the office. She was one of his best detectives but had a "hot dog" mentality and he couldn't afford to let her work the streets without the gentle giant, Kam, protecting her back. This didn't sit well with Cholly, and she'd been making everyone's lives miserable while she was confined to desk work. She greeted the news of a temporary new partner liked she'd heard she needed a root canal.

"What you need is to relax," replied the Captain. "When your new partner gets here, you can hit the streets again."

Cholly retorted, "I don't need a new partner. Kam'll be out of the hospital soon and in the meantime he can make calls from there."

The Captain sighed, "Listen, Hot Dog, you're not going out alone. And you're lucky; I hear this mainland sergeant is one ono cop, so be nice."

He picked up a folder and pushed it across the desk toward her. "This just came down from the Chief. I think you should look at it."

For lack of anything better to do, she flipped open the report and began reading. Despite herself, Cholly found the information interesting. She had to give the guy an "A" for variety but then a pattern jumped out at her. "Look, Rhodes scholar, law degree, licensed seaman, vice, narcotics, five commendations … but what are these gaps in time? Two months, then six months here, another more than a year?"

"Your guess is as good as mine, but I wonder if they were loaning him out," the Captain replied.

"And how can he transfer with rank?" A thorn in the side of many law enforcement officers was the fact that most often when they moved to another city, they could not keep their rank.

"That's none of your business," her boss replied. "You just show him the ropes and get on with solving your cases."

Of course Cholly had to admit, even if it was just to herself, that this guy could be Super Cop and she wouldn't want him. Ever since Kam, her oldest friend, and partner, had been injured two weeks ago, she'd been pestering the Captain to let her work alone. He had been adamantly opposed.

Breaking into her thoughts, the Captain asked her, "Anything new about the homicide victim they found at the Palace?"

Cholly shrugged, "You know they found Mr. Young in the moat below the concrete wall that faces the Palace windows. The preliminary investigation didn't turn up much except his brains were scrambled. He still seems to be what we found initially, a shoe salesman at Macy's. Quiet family man. I did find one problem; the wife's a kleptomaniac, but she's in therapy now and no one seems to be leaning on them."

"Have you found any connection between his being killed at Iolani Palace and the Sovereignty rally on the grounds that night?" he asked.

"Even though he was wearing a ceremonial cape, he isn't on any group's list and no one claims to know him. And since he still had his watch and wallet, it wasn't a robbery," she replied.

The Captain waved a photo of a pewter cup at her. "What have you found out about the cup that was under the body?"

"It's from the Palace but they have dozens of them; they're scattered around the displays in several of the rooms," she answered.

Their conversation was broken by the loud ringing of the phone. The Captain answered, listened, then slammed down the receiver. "There's another body, at the Mission Houses Museum, and guess what's next to it?"

"Don't tell me! A pewter cup. Just what I need, a double decker *and* a new partner!"

The wall clock chimed 8:30 and Cholly opened her mouth to make another remark when there was a knock on the glass top of the door. The Captain waved a hand and the door swung open. The dirty bum didn't come into the room, he just stood in the doorway.

Cholly's first reaction was that she'd been hit by a big jolt of electricity. Her second was that the man didn't need to walk into the room — he simply possessed it. She could feel his aura of sheer animal magnetism from where she sat. For a second Cholly felt as if he had sucked all the air out of the room.

This man had the body of a quarterback on a good day. The only thing keeping him from being drop-dead gorgeous was a once-broken nose. Powerful shoulders

8

topped a broad chest that strained against a torn and dirty T-shirt. His taut stomach looked like you could bounce a quarter on it.

But it was the view below the belt line that made Cholly swallow hard. He wore oil-streaked, white frayed jeans that fit like the skin on a Portuguese sausage. And she didn't need much imagination to know what was inside them. She'd bet a month's pay he wasn't wearing any underwear. If he were a woman, he'd have his own corner on Hotel Street!

Cholly disliked women or men who flaunted their sexuality, yet she couldn't keep her eyes from doing a head-to-toe inspection of this hunk.

The man moved over to shake hands with the Captain, not missing Cholly's scrutiny.

Captain Kahana stood to greet the man. "Morning, Hawkins, I'm glad to meet you. This is acting Lt. Kaloke Chan, but everyone calls her Cholly." And turning to Cholly, he continued, "And this is Sergeant Alexander Woodrow Hawkins III."

"Just call me Hawk," the man replied. His eyes were cold as blue crystals when they locked onto Cholly's soft brown ones. Finally, he broke off the look to do a number on her. He took his time sizing her up. Cholly couldn't decide whether he was thinking of buying her or eating her.

"Now that we're done taking inventory, perhaps we can get down to business, *Lieutenant,*" Hawk remarked sarcastically.

Cholly's face flushed under her honey-colored skin. Not only did he spell sex on the hoof, but he knew it.

9

Eying his getup with distaste, she retorted, "And just what business are you dressed for, *Sergeant?*"

The Captain interjected, "Hey, you're supposed to fight the bad guys, not each other."

Hawk moved over to the coffeepot, poured a cup and then sat down in the chair next to Cholly's. She wanted to move away, but wouldn't give him the satisfaction of knowing he bothered her.

The Captain asked him, "So how did your stakeout go?"

"Zilch. This lady, Aunty Noelani Lee, said her nephew Peter Jou was holing up down at the docks, but he was a no show," he replied.

Under her breath Cholly muttered, "He's not her nephew."

Hawk heard the comment. "But she said she was his aunt."

Cholly scoffed, "What she probably said was she's 'Aunty' Lee — that's not necessarily a relative."

The Captain sighed. "Now you see why I want you to partner up with Hawk, teach him the ropes, Hawaiian style."

Cholly, her tone laced with sarcasm, replied in the pidgin that natives often employed, "Wat I 'pose do with dis malahini?"

What little patience Hawk had left flew out the window. "Lady, don't do me any favors. I may not speak

Hawaiian, but I can usually figure things out. I've survived a long time in this business and I certainly don't need a babysitter."

The phone interrupted again. The Captain listened for a few minutes, grunted a reply, hung up and heaved himself out of his chair. "I have to go upstairs to the commissioner's office for a couple of minutes." He placed a folder marked, "Open Cases" in front of them. "Now you be good little kiddies and don't get any blood in the sandbox while I'm gone."

# Chapter 4

The two detectives left headquarters and headed straight to the Mission Houses Museum to investigate the newest death. The crime scene was taped off and personnel were working the area.

Cholly greeted Officer Peg Martin, then hunkered down next to the body and removed the wallet to check money and ID. "Who is it? He looks familiar."

Peg replied, "Mr. Polo, the playboy of the Winslow family. And it wasn't robbery. By the way, we found a typed note crumpled up near the body. It's going to the lab with the other evidence."

The women noted a slight commotion as Hawk approached the yellow tape line. Finally he ducked under the tape and moved toward them. His magnetism completely distracted them from the body. "That's my new partner," Cholly said in disgust.

Peg offered, "You can always throw him my way! Hmm, I don't see any underwear lines."

Overhearing her, Hawk replied, "That's because I'm not wearing any. I've been on surveillance all night and I didn't have time to go home and change."

Peg added an aside to Cholly, "Good thing you're not working undercover. But if things get too tough, I'll take him off your hands!"

Hawk kneeled down and rolled the body over. "Great, the bullet went clean through. Have they found it?"

"That would be too simple. There's a chance it's in the street. The team is getting metal detectors now," she answered.

"So who was he?" Hawk asked.

"One of the Winslows, a second company family … they were —" she started to reply.

"— Missionaries," he interrupted. She gave him a surprised look, and he added, "I'm from Boston."

"How did you transfer with rank?" she asked indignantly.

"None of your business," was the reply.

"Twice in one day, nice. Okay, Hot Shot, since I'm the primary on the case, you can do canvas. Go across the street to the church and find out if they heard anything last night," Cholly ordered.

Hawk hesitated, looking down at his dirty clothes. Cholly pointed him off with her chin and he shuffled away, trying to dust himself off. He crossed the street and walked near a non-descript figure wearing a large straw hat, and a baggy jacket and slacks. The person was leaning over one of the graves in the very small cemetery next to the church.

As the coroner's team removed the body on a gurney and placed it in the medical examiner's wagon, the person softly rasped, "Rot in peace, Kamuela."

Hawk didn't hear it; he had already entered the church. "And you couldn't tell if the caller was a man or a woman?" he was asking the church secretary.

"No, sir, the voice was hoarse, like laryngitis. The person wanted to know if there would be a wedding last night and if so, at what time," she answered.

"Was there a lot of music?" Hawk asked.

"Of course, Sergeant, this is Hawaii," she replied.

Hawk returned to the street to find reporters near the tape, calling out questions to Cholly. He walked over to her.

"Lt. Chan, is it true we have a serial killer on the loose?" a reporter asked.

"This investigation is just beginning —" she tried to answer.

Another reporter interrupted, "But there are two cups…. You've always played straight with us."

Hawk took Cholly's arm and parted the way for them to leave. "Sorry folks, but we have a date with the medical examiner," he announced.

He pulled her around the corner, where she immediately wrenched her arm loose and glared at him. "What the hell do you think you're doing?" she demanded.

"Helping you avoid questions you're not ready to answer," he said simply.

"In the future, keep your place," she glared.

"And where might that be, ma'am?" he replied.

"Two paces behind me!" Chin up, she began to march away.

# Chapter 5

As they left the reporters, the nondescript person from the cemetery stepped out from behind a tree. "Serial killer, eh? That might be interesting. Now I'm sorry I threw the gun into a dumpster."

---

The medical examiner still had not arrived. Hawk sighed and sagged down to lean against the wall. Cholly noted his movement and mentally remarked, "So, this is the big mainland hot shot. A few hours on stakeout and he wimps out like an old lady."

Aloud, she asked him, "What's the matter, Sergeant? The pace in Paradise too much for you?" She did a lousy job of hiding her sarcasm.

Hawk barely looked up at her. "No, ma'am, but I haven't eaten in 24 hours or slept in at least 36. The spirit is willing, but the flesh needs nourishment."

"Well, Number Three, your luck is changing. The dispatcher hasn't been able to reach anyone at the Winslow house, so we can grab a bit of breakfast," she answered with a smirk on her face and a little gleam in her eye.

"Great, but if it wouldn't be pushing my luck, I'd sure like to go back to the hotel and clean up first."

Cholly parked in front of the open air lobby at the Colony Surf to let Hawk out. Despite his slovenly appearance, female heads turned to watch him as he walked toward the elevator, a fact that wasn't lost on Cholly.

# Chapter 6

Their unmarked squad car pulled up in front of Bob's Saimen Bowl, more popularly referred to as the Black Hole. Cholly led Hawk, now in a Brooks Brothers suit, across a dilapidated patio with plastic booths. The cuts and tears in the seats had been repaired with assorted colors of vinyl tape.

Inside, the place looked even worse. Cholly surreptitiously watched Hawk's reaction to the dump. There were no actual tables, just non-working video games. On the left he saw a faded Formica counter with a back counter behind it. That one contained a stainless steel sink. An unbelievably high stack of dirty dishes towered over a sink of greasy gray water.

Cholly seated herself at the counter in front of this monument to filth. The stools were uncomfortably low for someone of Hawk's height, but he gamely stooped down and tried to get comfortable. Cholly slid a grease-stained menu toward him.

"You order," Hawk demurred.

A Chinese woman of about 40 came over to take their order. "Aloha, Min, we'll have two Loco Mocos," Cholly said. Then she continued in Chinese, requesting a "special order."

Min raised her eyebrows, then walked off shaking her head. She returned with coffee.

"Is this one of your favorite spots?" Hawk asked Cholly.

Biting back a smile, she nodded and gulped her coffee.

"Quaint," he replied.

Shortly, Aunty Ming Toy, a Chinese woman about 80, left the kitchen with a plate clutched in her claw-like hands. Her felt house slippers flip-flopped and she had to pause to wiggle them back on. Hawk watched her maneuver her way to the counter. She slid the plate down in front of him. It came a bit too fast and ended up stopping just in time, with the edge of the plate hanging over his crotch.

The plate held, in all its glory, a mound of dry, gray rice topped with a greasy hamburger that was draped in congealing brown gravy. A Portuguese sausage oozed grease next to a glob of green slime. Hawk glanced at it, then pushed it toward Cholly. "Ladies first," he said gallantly.

Cholly flashed a sugary smile, then insisted, "Oh, no, I wouldn't dream of it. You're starving! Enjoy."

Resignedly, Hawk began eating. After a few spoonfuls he decided it wasn't too bad, although he carefully avoided the slime. They heard the sound of a plate crashing to the floor, then a few moments later, Aunty Ming Toy reappeared and set a picture-perfect plate of bacon and eggs in front of Cholly. She muttered something to Cholly in Chinese and flip-flopped back to the kitchen.

Hawk looked at Cholly's dish, then his, then hers again. Cholly mumbled, "She dropped mine."

Once all his other food was gone, Hawk gingerly poked the slime with his spoon. "I think this has already been eaten," he commented as he took a taste. Despite herself, Cholly was a little impressed by his gamesmanship.

As they left the restaurant, Hawk grabbed Cholly's arm and pushed her up against the fender of the car. Through clenched teeth he announced, "Look, Lieutenant, you've had your fun. Game time is over. It's time to set some ground rules. If you can stop acting like a spoiled child and start acting like the professional you're supposed to be, perhaps we can get back to solving this murder case!"

"Oh lighten up, Number Three! I was just trying to loosen you up —" she began.

Just then, a cruiser pulled up and ended the altercation. As Hawk released Cholly's arm, the policeman in the car asked her in Japanese if she was all right. Rubbing her arm, Cholly answered that she and her new partner were just getting to know each other, perhaps a little too enthusiastically.

After the cruiser drove away, Cholly chided Hawk about his lack of humor. "And what assignment is so important that you're still here? This partnership is not going to work," she added.

Hawk replied, "It's probably a new concept to you, but in Boston, we follow the rules."

Cholly conceded, "We do the same in Honolulu, but we don't take ourselves too seriously. I'd suggest you not add starch to any of your clothes — you're already a stuffed shirt!"

Cholly was interrupted by her cell phone. "Hello? Yes, Mother, I know the Black and White Ball is — no, I don't have a date — obviously you haven't read the papers.

I'm up to my neck in a homicide investigation. *Mother*, you take care of the social obligations. Right now the victims are my priority!"

She punched the off button and gave Hawk a grimace. He started to make a wise-ass comment, then thought better of it.

# Chapter 7

Cholly and Hawk received word that Hiram Winslow was at his office, so they headed there.

The waiting room was furnished with items that looked as if they had been there since the day the company was founded. A dark brown leather couch and matching chairs filled one wall. A low cane table in front of them contained recent editions of several financial magazines. Placed around the room like sentinels were polished wooden pedestals topped with large green and brown glazed pots that were filled to overflowing with assorted ferns.

A rather dour-looking middle-aged woman sat behind a koa wood desk. She adjusted her horn-rimmed glasses and asked that they state their business.

Cholly displayed her card and badge case. "I'm Lieutenant Chan and this is Sergeant Hawkins. We would like to see Hiram Winslow."

"May I ask what your business —"

"No, you may not. Please ...." Hawk pointed meaningfully at the intercom.

In contrast to the almost cramped waiting room, Hiram Winslow's office was spacious. It, too, was a monument to history. Framed photos and a boar's head were mounted on the walls, while sailing trophies and almost every conceivable type of memento was scattered on tables or attached to the walls.

Hiram Winslow sat behind a huge mahogany desk that seemed to dwarf the 50-ish looking man. Pale skinned for someone who lives in the tropics, his watery blue eyes enhanced the effect. He ran slightly-trembling, stubby fingers through his almost white hair.

He turned his attention to Hawk. "What can I do for you, Lieutenant?"

Hawk had to hide a smile as Cholly almost snapped, "I'm Lieutenant Chan. This is Sergeant Hawkins."

Winslow shrugged off the faux pas. "What can I do for you, officers?"

"I'm afraid we have some bad news for you, sir. Your brother, Kamuela, is dead."

Cholly watched him carefully. It was a given in law enforcement that many homicides were committed by friends or relatives, so she wanted to monitor his reaction to what should be shocking news.

Winslow sat rigid, no emotion, eyes staring, hands gripping the edge of the desk.

Hawk took a step closer to the desk. "Sir?"

Slowly the watery eyes focused on him. He opened his mouth to speak but no words came out. Hawk stepped around behind him and poured a glass of water from a carafe on the credenza. He placed it in the older man's hand and raised it upwards. Winslow took a sip, then seemed to come to life.

His voice was low as he croaked out the first word. "What?" After a pause, the words suddenly poured out. "When — where — how did it happen?"

Cholly filled him in on the details, then took out her notebook. "I know this is a difficult time for you, Mr. Winslow, but we need to ask you some questions. In a case of homicide, it's very important for us to move quickly."

He hesitated a second, then agreed. "Of course; ask anything you feel you need to."

"Do you know what he was doing at the Mission Houses Museum at night?"

"I have no idea. I think I should start, Lieutenant, by telling you that except for business or random social functions, I do not — did not — see my brother very often."

"Why is that, sir?" Hawk's voice was matter of fact.

"What do you mean? Why do I have to explain —"

"Mr. Winslow, I believe what the Sergeant is getting at is that most families have some contact on a regular basis. And he did live at the family home —"

"He did not."

Hawk looked at his notebook. "According to his driver's license —"

"Let me clarify the situation. He did live with me until about six months ago. Then he moved out and purchased a condo."

It was obvious that Cholly's attitude offended Winslow and he wasn't shy about saying so.

"Why?" Cholly's tone was suspicious. "Look, Mr. Winslow, I'll make this very simple. We are investigating a homicide. When it comes to murder, we don't have a sense of humor, nor do we play games. We are, of course, sorry for your loss, and are sure you want us to do everything we can to apprehend your brother's murderer. Now we have every reason to be curious as to why a 42-year-old man who has always lived in the old family mansion suddenly decides to move out."

The fight seemed to go out of Winslow and he nodded in agreement. "For many years we had been at loggerheads about his spending habits — mainly his string of polo ponies." He paused and put his head in his hands as if trying to regain his composure.

Hawk and Cholly stood quietly, waiting for him to continue.

"I'm sorry, but this has been such a shock."

"We understand, sir. Take your time. But when you feel up to continuing, would you tell us if those were the only problems you two had?"

He seemed to weigh his thoughts before answering. "It is hard to discuss such personal things. And you must remember what I have to tell you is confidential."

"Of course."

"Like all the other plantation owners, we are having a difficult time because of the cane and pine decline. We still run a lot of cattle on the Big Island," his hand swept a grandiose gesture, "and of course have our real estate properties in Honolulu, but it has been necessary to cut back on some of the things that have always been a part of our family's lifestyle."

"What has that to do with your brother moving out?"

"We were constantly arguing about his spending habits. He is — was — 10 years younger, born rather late to my parents. They, and our father in particular, always indulged him. He had absolutely no sense of the value of money."

"If money was tight, how could he afford to buy a condo?" Hawk had taken on the role of "good cop," playing his questions soft and sympathetic

"Kamuela had a monthly income from a separate trust fund."

"Did he actively work in the business?"

Winslow's laugh brought chills down Cholly's spine. If had a quality ranging between hatred, disgust, and ended with a hint of absurdity. "Work?! Kamuela's idea of work was deciding what party invitation to accept and what to wear."

"But, sir, you did mention you saw him for business reasons."

"Only when his presence was necessary to sign papers or something of that nature."

"I'm sure through the years that must have been a problem for you," Hawk remarked.

"I know where you're going with this, Sergeant, but you're wrong. Actually, it was a blessing. I was free to do as I pleased; run things the way father wanted."

"Mr. Winslow, would you please prepare a list of his acquaintances for us? Also, is this the address of the stable where his horses were kept?" asked Cholly as she handed him the business card Hawk had found in the dead man's wallet.

Winslow nodded and said, "I think so. He was always arguing with vendors. I seem to remember his moving the ponies a time or two."

"And are there any other people you think we should talk to?"

"No, I can't help you there. I don't really know who his friends were, other than those from the polo and country clubs"

"Did he have a girlfriend, someone special that you knew about?"

"He used to fancy himself a playboy, but you'll have a better chance of finding out that type of information from his horse friends."

"Just for the record, where were you last night, Mr. Winslow?" queried Cholly.

"Surely you could not possibly think I had anything to do with my brother's death?" Hiram replied indignantly.

Hawk soothed him, "Sir, it's just a routine question. Will you please give the lieutenant an answer."

"I was at home," he replied.

"Were you alone?" asked Hawk.

"Yes, except for my houseman, but he was in his quarters. And just for the record, I resent your asking me such a question," was the response.

They moved toward the door, then Cholly stopped, turned and asked as if it was an afterthought, "To your knowledge, Mr. Winslow, did your brother have any enemies?"

He hesitated a second, then gave her a shrug and a half smile. "Don't we all?"

The two exited Winslow's office, discussing their encounter with the "bereaved" brother.

"Well, does he fit your profile of a grief-stricken relative?" Hawk asked Cholly.

"He sure is a cold fish, but I hear he is the brains of the organization so he probably resented the playboy sharing the loot," she answered.

"Enough to kill him?" Hawk asked.

"Money still makes one of the best motives," she replied.

"Who's going to dig into it?" he asked.

"Get a shovel," she snapped. "Let's head to the morgue.

# Chapter 8

The morgue was not exactly a cheery place. Three walls were tiled and the fourth was filled with stainless steel drawers. A cloth-covered body with a tagged toe sticking out was lying on a gurney in the middle of the room when they entered. Otherwise the room was empty, although country music was blaring from behind a partition.

Cholly called out, "Hey, Doc, you here?"

A middle-aged Japanese man appeared from behind the panel carrying a plate with white and pink squishy globs that looked like something left over from an autopsy. He was dressed in western wear and doing his best to act like John Wayne — and failing.

"Ohayo gozaimasu, Tanaka-san," Cholly greeted the man.

Yoshi Tanaka gave her a puzzled look, then responded, "Ohayo gozaimasu." He bowed toward Hawk, then extended the plate, first to Cholly then Hawk. Hawk hesitated, but after Cholly took one of the pieces and bit into it, Hawk reluctantly selected the smallest piece.

"Oh, Doc, these are awful!" Cholly exclaimed.

He agreed, "You got that right 'pardner.' It's my daughter's first attempt at making mochi — but have another."

"Forget it! I hate mochi, even on a good day," Cholly answered.

Pointing to Cholly, Dr. Tanaka turned to Hawk. "The woman has no soul. You must be Hawkins. I hope you can survive working with her. Do you know what happened to her other partner?"

"I heard he broke his hip but I didn't know it was her fault," he replied.

Cholly burst in, "It wasn't! We were chasing a perp. Kam took the back and jumped out of what he thought was a first-floor window."

"But it wasn't?" Hawk asked.

"Yeah, in the front of the house. But the lot sloped down. In the back it was the second floor." She paused. "Okay, Doc, lose the treats and let's see what your corpse has to tell us."

Tanaka started to turn on the microphone, then stopped and went back to a desk. He returned and handed several pictures to Hawk. He then started the post-mortem, keeping up a steady stream of conversation as he worked.

"Those large pictures are the crime scene photos of the first victim. I took the smaller ones last night," Tanaka explained. "Hey, guys, guess what, that first stiff died twice!"

"Excuse me, Tonto, but how does someone die twice?" Cholly asked.

"Well, first his head was smashed open like a melon," Tanaka answered. He grinned at Hawk. "Hope I'm not being too technical for you, Sergeant," he continued.

"I'll try to keep up," responded Hawk.

"Anyway, the uniforms thought he died in the fall, but when I started probing around behind his ear, I found an entry wound," said Tanaka as with a flourish he pulled a bullet out of an envelope lying on the tray. He dropped it into a metal basin.

Continuing, Tanaka said, "How much you wanna bet it'll match the bullet that took care of victim number two?"

Cholly replied, "Assuming we ever find the damn thing."

# Chapter 9

The detectives' next stop was to visit the deceased's home at the address Winslow had given them. It was a small, but nice house furnished with high class tropical items. Officers were already at the site, looking into the bedroom, kitchen, opening drawers. Cholly looked thoroughly through the desk drawers. In a corner of the living room an alcove had been converted into a bar.

When Hawk moved around behind the bar, he discovered several photos mounted on the side wall. One of them was of four people: the dead man and his brother, an older woman, and another man in the background. The setting looked like a winners' circle at a horse show.

"Hey, Boss Lady," Hawk called to Cholly, "take a look at this." As she moved over to look, he continued, "Why would a man who says he doesn't know anything about his brother or his horse hobby end up at one of the meets?"

Studying the photo, Cholly replied, "That's a pretty fancy trophy; maybe it was one of the big charity shows."

"Do you recognize the other man and the woman?" Hawk asked her.

"I've never seen the guy. The lady looks slightly familiar but I can't put a name to the face," she admitted.

"Did you find anything important in the desk?" he asked.

"Not really. Mostly horse-related papers, some bills," she said.

"Paid, or did he have money problems?" Hawk wondered.

Flipping through the papers in her hand, Cholly responded, "They all seem to be current, but we'll check them out when we get back to the office." She looked around to see if she was missing anything, then walked back to the desk to press the play button on the blinking answering machine.

A voice said, "Hey, Mr. Winslow, this is Bill over at the leather shop. Your bridle is done; let us know if you want to pick it up or if we should have it delivered to the stable."

"On the surface, it doesn't seem like he had any major problems," Hawk observed.

To Cholly's raised eyebrow he replied, "Yeah, I know, keep digging.

# Chapter 10

As they were driving back to the office, Cholly in the driver's seat noticed Hawk leaning back and almost asleep. She decided he'd had enough and headed over to the Colony Surf. Hawk woke up when the car stopped in front.

"What are we doing here?" he asked in confusion.

"You're out on your feet. I'll finish up for today; you get some sleep," she offered.

"Thanks, er, mahalo! I really do need to sack out. Meet you at 8 a.m. tomorrow, okay?" Hawk said as he gratefully climbed out of the car. Cholly drove off and Hawk headed into the lobby.

The desk clerk handed Hawk his key and a phone message slip. In his room, Hawk looked at the note, frowned, and made a phone call. Speaking in Mandarin, he said, "Yellow Bird, it's me. Where ….?" Continuing in English, he said, "When? Are you sure?"

He had no sooner hung up than his phone rang. The demanding voice on the other end belonged to Allyson, Hawk's ex-fiancée. "I miss you so much, darling. If you really loved me, you'd come back home," she sulked at him.

He sighed. "I miss you, too, Allyson, but it's too late for us. I don't plan to change for you. I will always be a cop and that's a problem. And anyway, I'm on assignment and I can't leave right now."

"Oh, Woodrow, if you need money, you know Daddy would be more than happy to —"

He cut her off. "Look, I'm not working for anyone's father, famous lawyer or not. I hope you have a good trip to Bangkok, but I've gotta go."

Her protest was cut off as he hung up the phone, and plopped facedown on the bed. He was asleep in seconds.

---

Back at headquarters, Cholly stood adding a photo to the evidence board. Standing in the doorway of his office, the Captain asked, "Where's Hawkins?"

"I sent him home," replied Cholly.

Annoyed, the Captain responded, "Cholly, I warned you …."

"It's not like that. The guy was out on his feet," she explained.

"Okay. What did you find out about the cups?" he queried.

"I already told you, we'll know more when the curator gets back tomorrow," she answered.

# Chapter 11

Hawk tossed and turned in his hotel bed, then awoke with a start. Confused, he got out of bed and walked to the window. Below he saw people eating dinner on the Outrigger Club lanai. He took a few steps toward the shower, then changed his mind, sat down on the bed and made a phone call.

Hailing a cab, he headed to the hospital and found his way to Kam Alpa's room. Kam reclined in his hospital bed. "Come on in and take a load off, brah," invited the enormous man. He motioned to a chair piled high with books. "Just put dat stuff on the floor. I spoke with Cholly a while ago, she sounded pupule."

Kam broke off two apple bananas from a small stalk resting on his nightstand. He tossed one to Hawk, then peeled the other one; it was gone in one bite.

Hawk fingered the yellow speckled skin and let out a resigned sigh. "And what does pupule mean?"

Kam paused, then gave Hawk his most ingratiating smile. "Crazy, but the nice kind. You know, no strait jackets or dat da kine."

"I wouldn't bet on that," Hawk answered. Then he hesitated. He didn't know what kind of relationship Kam and Cholly had. "Your ... ah ... friend is certifiable."

The big Hawaiian's laugh richoted around the walls. "I hear she's been giving you a real hard time."

"That's an understatement. What's with her?"

34

"My 'Little Rose,' she's always marched to her own drummer. All time different. Maybe it's the Chinese in her. She used ta wish she was born a boy. Her dad one strange kane. He gives her funny name and gets mad when she won't go into the family business. Then says it's okay to be detective like Uncle. Only now they give her a hard time 'cause she won't get married and have kids Go figure."

"What's with 'Little Rose'? Doesn't she have enough names already?"

Again, Kam's laugh filled the room. "By golly, you got that right, but that's just my pet name for her. Kaloke means rose, too."

"The problem is this rose has thorns."

Silence filled the room. Despite Kam's outgoing, almost buffoonish manner, there lay behind it a very shrewd mind. He wanted to know more about this Hawkins guy, the man who could hold Cholly's life in his hands. And Kam had a gut feeling that maybe the new guy might soon be developing more than a casual interest in his best friend.

Kam took a gulp from a can of cola. "Joking aside, how you getting long? It's got to be a tough adjustment." His tone registered genuine interest and Hawk let down his natural reserve.

Thoughtfully, he rubbed the back of his neck before answering. "That's probably the all-time understatement. I've seen my share of the world and can always find a way to fit in, but I usually don't have to deal with …." He threw his hands up. How could he explain his frustration to Kam? He smiled at the huge figure dwarfing the hospital bed; the guy could probably stop a locomotive with one hand.

"Cholly?"

"She resents having to work with me and doesn't bother to hide her feelings; she uses sarcasm like a hair shirt."

"She's a real piece of work, all right. Wait 'til you hear some of the stories the vice guys tell."

Taking the opening Kam gave him, Hawk commented, "Maybe if I knew a little about her, I could figure out a way to handle her."

"If you do, I hope you'll share it with me!" Kam quickly warmed to the subject and Hawk noted the pure love shining in Kam's eyes. In a vague sort of way that bothered him, but he didn't dwell on the idea.

"When I met her, she was about 10 and had just been thrown out of Punahoo —that's a fancy private school. She came over to Kamehameha school —"

"Hold it a minute! How does a little kid get thrown out of school?"

"Actually, it was the second school she'd been to. See the problem was Cholly had her own sense of right and wrong and always acted on it. Didn't matter if she was the runt of the litter, if she saw a big kid picking on a smaller one, she'd jump right in. Now, nice little girls, especially from high-class families, don't do that kind of thing. And if big mouth didn't think a teacher was right on some point of Hawaiian history, she'd correct them." Although Kam shook his head at the memories, it was obvious to Hawk that he was proud of Cholly.

"How did she become such a pint-sized authority?"

"Her Tutu — that's a grandma. She's a Kahuna, that's like a high priest. Her Hawaiian family big-time people. All plenty smart on both sides. Going to college ain't enough, they got to have half the alphabet after their names."

"So how'd you two meet?"

Kam's pearl white teeth shown like a spotlight against his bronzed skin. "How do you think?"

Almost in unison they chorused, "In a fight!"

"A playground bully swiped a little kid's lunch money. The kid stood there crying. The bully was laughing at him when Cholly wiped the smile off his face. Or at least she tried to. She was on the ground with a bloody nose when I stepped in and finished the job."

"And you've been the dynamic duo ever since?"

"Are you kidding? The last thing I needed while I was trying to be a teenage stud was to have some puny little kid tagging after me. Trust me, brah, I tried like hell to avoid her."

"Obviously you weren't successful."

"Finally, I got desperate and went to her house. Figured the last thing a family like hers would want was for her to be hanging out with a big kanaka. A maid opened the door and told me no one was home except "Miss Kaloke" who was out in the garden. I go around back and there's Shorty curled up and crying in one of them gazebo things."

"What was the matter?"

"Her folks were at the end of their rope. They didn't know what to do with her; the boys were models of polite perfection, never caused trouble, knew their place, all dat crap. Don't get me wrong, Hawkins, kids got to behave but the problem was Cholly doesn't fit in any mold that's been invented."

Hawk could picture the pathetic little face, bewildered by what she was doing wrong, when in fact all she was doing was being herself. The view seemed to change and suddenly he could see a young boy's face instead of hers. The face was his own. Quickly, he forced his thoughts back to the present.

"What was she upset about?"

"Her folks had taken off to see about putting her in boarding school on the mainland, but her grandfather wanted them to send her to school in China. Anyway, we talked for hours; she really spilled her guts. I got the feeling it was first time anyone ever really listened to what she had to say, what she was feeling."

Some of Kam's speech hit close to home, but Hawk shook off his mood. "Sounds pretty heavy duty for a teenage stud."

"Yeah, but ... see, I come from a big family — happy — noisy — we fight — we make up. And here was this little rich kid with nothing; I mean nada, zippo."

"So what did you do?"

"I went to her folks and told them I'd be responsible for her, to give her another semester to get her act together."

"And they agreed?"

"After about having a heart attack when they met me!"

"That must have been the semester from hell."

"It turned out to be simple. I've always been big for my age and pointed out to her how important it was to learn to stay in control." Kam drew himself upright and took on a fake cultured tone. "I said I couldn't afford to lose my temper. I know it sounds corny, but it worked. And we developed a code; all I had to do was say "Irish" and she'd back off."

"Is that more Island lingo?"

"Naw, I just meant don't get your Irish up."

Hawk nodded sheepishly. "In one day I've had the rough side of her tongue and been treated to her slightly weird sense of humor. I guess I want to know what to expect next — or maybe just how to deal with Robo Cop."

Kam took a beat to consider how to answer Hawk. As her best friend and biggest fan, he was well aware that she could be a pain in the okole. "You kinda hit the nail on the head with the Robo Cop da kine. To get where she wanted to be, Cholly's had to hang tough, make a lot of sacrifices."

"Why?" asked Hawk.

"For openers, she's 'Chop Suey' — a mix of Hawaiian, Chinese and Scottish. That makes her pupule," Kam began. Off Hawk's look, he continued, "You know, crazy sometimes. Pake family say, 'You be banker like rest of us, be more lady-like.' Hawaiian side say 'hang loose, have fun, too.'"

"What happened to the Scottish part?" Hawk asked.

Kam sighed and hesitated again. It was obvious his feelings for her ran high.

"I think the only time she ever had fun as a kid was the summers she spent on the Big Island at the cattle ranch that belonged to her Scottish uncle, Malcolm.

"What changed that?" Hawk wondered

"When she got to be an older teenager, every summer she had to go to work in one of the family banks in Hong Kong," Kam told him.

"That's some stretch to being a cop," Hawk commented.

"She had to fight for that, too. They gave her three years to prove herself. If she didn't, she'd go to work in the bank," Kam explained.

"Looks like the joke's on them," said Hawk.

"Yeah, but they ain't laughing. They still on her back on that social da kine," Kam said, shaking his head in disgust. Then he offered Hawk a box of candy.

# Chapter 12

When Cholly picked Hawk up the next morning, he asked her to swing by an apartment complex first. He was considering moving there and needed to check out the available apartment. The apartment manager unlocked the door, then left them to look the place over.

"Well, Boss Lady, what do you think? It's not very big, but don't you think it has a great deal of charm?"

Living arrangements were the last thing on her mind at the moment. She was shocked to discover herself physically reacting to his body, and her reply was a distracted nod.

To change the subject, he asked, "Just out of curiosity, Lieutenant, how come you still wear your blues? Most of us can't wait to get out of them."

"You wouldn't understand," she answered brusquely.

"Try me."

"Authority." The single word hung there. Finally, in answer to the questioning look he gave her, she continued. "Look, the perps are often a head taller or have 75-100 pounds on me."

With a chuckle, Hawk said, "So, you're human after all!"

The jibe was lost on her. Cholly's body was reacting like a school girl on her first date. Feeling she had to move away from him, Cholly turned, forgetting Hawk was right behind her. She bumped into his chest. It was like hitting a stone wall. For a micro-second, a wave of intimacy sparked between them. Then they both quickly stepped back, muttering inane remarks about the fact that it was already getting late, they had an appointment and forensics to check on, and other lies to cover their surprised reaction to each other.

---

Simon Collins, curator of Iolani Palace, sat behind his desk, talking to Cholly and Hawk. He looked to be about 60, sporting leonine white hair and bronze skin. It was clear that he was finding the conversation very stressful. The pewter cups found at the murder scenes sat in front of him on his desk.

"Mr. Collins, do you have any idea how Mr. Young could have gotten hold of a cup?" Cholly asked.

"He might have stolen it from a display, although most of these cups are in storage," he answered.

"In a vault?"

"No, it's not really necessary," he answered. "While they are old, we're not talking about a great deal of monetary value."

"And you're sure you don't know Mr. Young?" she continued.

"As I said, he may be a member, but unless he was someone, like your family, Lieutenant, I wouldn't have any contact with him," he replied.

"But you did know Kamuela Winslow?" she asked.

"Of course, although not very well. It's his brother, Hiram, who is our patron," he said.

"How do you explain the fact that two cups from your collection have shown up at the murder sites?" Hawk demanded.

"I assure you, Sergeant, I have no idea," he insisted.

Cholly thoughtfully commented, "Unless …."

Collins mopped his brow. "Are you suggesting that someone connected with the Palace is involved in these crimes?"

"Two cups, two murders, only a few blocks apart. I think maybe it's time we found out more about where everyone was Tuesday night," Cholly said.

Hawk gave Collins a little smile. "And since we're here, we might as well start with you."

# Chapter 13

After dropping some evidence off at forensics, they went back to the office. While waiting for a call from Washington, Hawk found out additional information about the first murder victim, Mr. Young. Several shoplifting complaints had been lodged against Mrs. Young. However, no one had pressed charges when she agreed to go into counseling.

He told Cholly what he'd learned and she said, "Well, that ties in with some hints I've been getting from a few neighbors. Did you get your call yet?"

"No." He looked at the clock on the wall, "It's after five in Washington."

"Well, maybe it wasn't too important."

Hawk let out a deep breath. "Yeah, right." But he knew better.

The Captain called them in to his office so they could give him an update on the two murders. "What do you have so far?"

Hawk responded, "When I talked to the people at the church, two things came up. The secretary had what she felt was a very unusual call earlier in the day. The person wanted to know what time the wedding service was being held, and would there be music."

"The person? Didn't she know if it was a man or a woman?"

"No. The voice was muffled … had a grating sound … like someone with laryngitis."

"And what was the second thing? I hope it's something more concrete."

"Yes and no. At the reception afterwards, one of the guests remarked to the rector that she was surprised to see someone going onto the grounds of the Mission Houses. She made quite an issue of it — a woman alone, wandering around in such a dark, deserted area."

"A woman? You're not going to tell me our perp was a woman?"

"I don't think the wedding guest was that sure, but she thought she saw what looked like a dark muu'muu."

"Well, it's better than nothing. Maybe you'll have more luck at the stable."

# Chapter 14

"I thought I had seen some beautiful polo grounds, but this tops everything, Chan." The partners were on their way to the stables where Kamuela Winslow boarded his horses. In order to get there, they had to pass one of the playing fields. The lush green land sat literally on the shore line. In some places, there was less than twenty feet of white sand, a band of ironwood trees and the field itself. The gentle rolling surf and cobalt sky became a picturesque background for the area.

"It is kind of awesome. I had a friend who liked the polo matches. We'd come out and picnic on the edge between the field and the shore: champagne, pate — "

Hawk's raised eyebrow stopped Cholly's recitation. "What? You don't think I have the ability to be cosmopolitan?"

"No, it's not that. I guess I would have figured you more for fried chicken or laulau."

"If you had let me finish, I was going to add sushi."

Hawk let out a triumphant laugh. "That's my girl."

The car crunched up the gravel road and Hawk parked in the shade of a cluster of palm trees. The stable itself was a low concrete building with a tin roof. Bright green stall doors, split so the top half opened, ran along one wall. The graceful heads of several horses emerged as they walked by.

The exercise area in front of the building was encircled with a white fence. Two horses were tethered to a mechanical hot walker. They moved in a slow circle, glanced at the approaching officers, whinnied a welcome and went on with their walk.

Cholly draped herself over the top rail and studied the animals. One was a jet black stallion, the other a gorgeous chestnut gelding. Their height was at least 16 hands, and they were a picture of strength and beauty.

"They just take your breath away," she said as her eyes took on an almost radiant look of appreciation. "You can just feel their power —"

"Do you like to ride?"

"I tried it as a kid but I didn't like it."

First Hawk's jaw dropped a fraction, then he slapped his forehead in mock amazement. "Well, hallelujah, I finally found something you can't do! I've got to circle this on my calendar, this is certainly a red-letter day."

She pulled a face at him. "Very funny, Number Three." She undraped herself and moved toward the building. "Let's go play detective."

A true paniolo type wandered out of the barn. His jeans had seen better days, but his blue-and-white-denim palaka shirt looked fairly new. The man was in his early 60s, his face lined from years of squinting into the sunlight. A sweat-stained cowboy hat with a brown feathered headband perched over short gray hair. He wore leather gloves and was coiling a lead line in his hands.

"Morning. You the cops?"

"Yes, sir, this is Lieutenant Chan, I'm Sergeant Hawkins."

"I'm Mac Morales, the owner. Come on in the office; we'll grab a cup of coffee."

He led the way back to the barn and entered a door just inside the opening of the overhead doors.

The sweet aroma of straw was mixed with the usual, if subtle, ammonia odor, but the area was spotless and the tack that hung outside each stall was well polished and expensive looking.

A dented metal coffecpot sat on an electric hot plate. Morales passed the cups around, brushed the inevitable thin layer of barn dust off a small leather couch and gestured for them to sit down.

Cholly looked around at the trophies and blankets adorning the walls and filling the shelves on a side wall. "It looks like your horses do quite well."

"Can't complain. Been in the business 40 years so you collect a lot of junk. 'Course some of these belong to my boarders.

"Speaking of boarders, what can you tell us about Kamuela Winslow?"

"What you want to know?"

Hawk fought a wry smile. It seemed cowboys were laconic no matter where they lived. He took out his notebook and pen. "For starters, how long has he boarded with you?"

"Oh, about seven years, ever since he got into the polo game."

The detectives had a mutual reaction of surprise at this piece of news. That timeframe contradicted Hiram Winslow's comment.

Morales continued, "He started on their ranch on the Big Island, but brought some of his stock over here. After a year or so, he sent them all to Oahu."

"Was he a good client?"

"In what way?"

"Umm, pay his bills, get along with the help, you know, that kind of thing," Cholly added.

"A few times he was late, but that's 'cause he was off island. But usually it was like clockwork."

"Polo's an expensive hobby. Did he ever complain about the charges, or question them?" Hawk's tone was very casual, but they could both see Morales bristle at the last part of the question.

"You asking me if he thought I cheated him?"

"Not necessarily, sir, but with six horses, well, a lot of times there can be things like duplicate charges, accidentally, of course."

"No, Sergeant, we got along just fine. There were a few problems couple years back. A new vet from the mainland got pretty cute with some of his charges, but that was strictly 'tween him and Winslow. I don't get into that stuff."

"What about your staff. How did he get along with them?"

"Ain't got no staff really. My boy mucks out the stalls after school. Got one part-timer, Keo McGreagor."

"What does he do the rest of the time?"

"Drives a cab in Honolulu, mostly at night, but some day shifts too. He and Winslow got along fine."

Cholly pressed on. "What was Winslow's relationship with the other team members? Any problems?"

"I mind my own business, Lieutenant."

"But Mr. Winslow was your business, Mr. Morales. You have to have had a slight interest in what happened to a man whose horses fill half of your barn."

Morales hesitated, obviously uncomfortable, but then shrugged his shoulders as if realizing he had no choice but to answer Cholly's question. "A few times I took his horses to matches when Keo couldn't work. He seemed to get along with people pretty good — except —"

"Except what?" Hawk interrupted.

"He was a bad winner. You know the kind: rub your nose in it. The locals kinda ignored him, but some of the visiting teams really got pissed off — excuse me ma'am."

"I've heard the word before, Mr. Morales. So, he did have a few enemies —"

"Aw, I wouldn't call them enemies, least not the killin' kind if that's what you're saying."

"What about his brother, Hiram? Did he ever come out here, or go to the matches?"

50

"Not that I know of. Winslow used to say his brother bitched about the costs, but that's all I know about him."

They drove away in silence, each one running the interview through their mental computers. Eventually Cholly asked, "What's your opinion?"

"Sounds like he was a typical spoiled playboy type."

She couldn't resist: "Like some of your friends?"

He ignored her, a habit he was trying to develop. "Some of those boys get into heavy side betting. That might be an angle to check out, but I don't think he had any serious problems with the stable people."

# Chapter 15

As he eased the car back down the lane and onto the highway, Hawk asked, "Where to now?"

She glanced through the sheets in her notebook. "Let's go back to the Palace. I checked, and all the docents will be on duty about now. Let's ask them if they remember anyone acting suspicious. After all, those cups didn't just walk out by themselves."

When they pulled into the driveway of the Palace, Hawk asked, "How long do you think it will take to question the docents who were on duty Saturday?"

"We should be out of here in 30 minutes, maybe less. According to this list the Curator gave me, there are only four of them, two men and two women. Hello, look whose name is on the list, the last one!"

Hawk looked over her shoulder at the note. "Hiram Winslow. I wonder why he didn't mention that he's a docent?"

"Who knows? We'll make a note of it."

"In the meantime, did they all have access to the room where the Missionary Collection is kept?"

Cholly glanced in her notebook. "Actually, the Collection is displayed throughout several rooms in the Palace; so the killer could have taken it from any one of them."

"Great, that sure narrows it down, doesn't it."

They were interviewing the last docent, Winslow. So far, none of them had seen anything out of the ordinary. And to their knowledge, nothing had been removed.

"So, during your tours no one made a move to touch anything, pick something up and look it over?"

An indignant, "Absolutely not," almost filled the room. "Our docent training teaches us how to be on the alert for such movements. After all, Sergeant, these items are priceless, historically speaking. Nothing was disturbed during my tours, I can assure you."

"Well, that was a wasted 34 minutes," Hawk remarked as he slid behind the wheel of the blue and white."

"Uh, you're right. But —"

"But what?"

"I don't know. I can't put my finger on it; it's that funny little itch I get when I feel something isn't kosher."

---

Before the detectives left, the killer slipped into a tower room, then watched as their police car pulled away. A sly smile played at the corners of normally grim lips. "The fools — they never suspected they could reach out and touch their adversary."

# Chapter 16

"Hey, Ipo, I may have a break for you," Kam sounded so excited, his voice boomed over the phone line.

"I could sure use a break, Ipo. What's up?"

"You know my snitch, Gus, who hangs out near the docks, the guy who can't write?"

"Sure."

"He got a message to me. Says he knows something about your stiffs. He wanted me to meet him, but I sent word for him to come to the hospital. Then he replied that I should send you to meet him at the Rose Bar around five. A $20 usually satisfies him unless he asks for more in advance."

Cholly hesitated, warning bells sounding in her brain. That bar was definitely not a place for nice girls, especially without Kam. But what worried her the most was Kam's man offering to sell her something. Snitches normally wouldn't do business with anyone but their contact, so why was he suddenly being so out of character?

"Hey, Ipo, you still there?"

"Yeah," came back in a very flat tone of voice.

"Well, don't blind me with your radiant enthusiasm, partner. Here I thought you'd be jumping for joy, or something."

"It smells, Kam. Why does he come out of the woodwork to do me a favor?"

"It's no favor, it's strictly cash and carry. He's probably broke as usual."

"And at Rose's bar, yet. I hope my will is up to date."

"It'll still be daylight, and you'll have Hawkins with you." Kam suddenly didn't sound as cheerful as he had at the beginning of their conversation. "Look, if you really have reservations about this, give it a miss. I'll put out the word you can't make it and to meet you some place safe — maybe the zoo or aquarium."

"Great, a junkie wouldn't stick out too much there, would he, Alpa?"

"Hey, gimme a break. I'm trying to do you a favor. What more do you want from me, Ipo?"

Cholly apologized, then added, "This whole thing stinks. And having to work with Hawkins the Third doesn't make it any better."

"Cholly, why don't you back off and give him a chance? We both know Cap wouldn't have paired him up with you if he thought the guy couldn't handle it."

"You're right; I guess I'm just strung out today."

"Well, brush up your Tagalog and go get 'em, Tiger."

---

"Are you sure this is the smart thing to do? Most snitches will only talk to their contact. If this guy belongs to Kam —"

55

"Do me a favor, Hawkins, and just drive." Cholly's voice was tight and that fact wasn't lost on him. What was her problem now?

"When you get to Bethel Street, pull into the parking lot."

Hawk edged the car into the last parking space, then looked around. He didn't see any bar named "Club Rose" — there wasn't a bar, period. He started to get out of the car but she raised her hand to stop him. "You stay here. This won't take a minute."

"Hey, from what you told me, this is the kind of place you can get your head handed to you. There's no way I'll let you go in alone."

"And how far do you think I'd get with you tagging along, Blondie? Stay!" She walked to the end of the lot and moved into the alley.

Hawk watched her stiffen up, roll her shoulders back and move her holster a fraction closer to her hand. "There are thousands of officers in HPD and I have to get paired up with Robo Cop," he complained to himself as he checked his watch, trying to decide just how long he would give her.

Cholly moved slowly through the dim alley. Although it was still afternoon, the building across the way threw heavy shadows into the passage. She ignored the back door of the club and slid around the corner in order to enter through the front. Again she straightened up, said a little prayer, touched her gun to reassure herself it was there, and pushed open the peeling door.

The afternoon sunlight cut into the dark room like a bright spotlight. The bar babble stopped within seconds as the crowd began checking her out. Her training officer had taught her that in situations like this, she should start her gaze at one side and sweep the room, trying to make eye contact with as many people as possible. It was a tool to give one time to assess the situation and make them think you're in control.

As Cholly's eyes panned the group, two things registered with her. First, there didn't seem to be a hostess, nor was there an actual bar. Second, she couldn't see Gus anywhere. The brief snippets of conversations she had caught when she entered reminded her that this was a Filipino club and the customers were speaking Tagalog. She knew fewer than two dozen words. Some days, it just didn't pay to get out of bed.

Most of the 40 or so patrons appeared to be in their late 20s or 30s. A young man, his face scarred and set with a feral gleam, stood up.

"Umi opo ka, naman," Cholly ordered, and the man hesitated. Instead of sitting down, he glanced at a woman standing to the side.

The woman, who looked to be about 50, stood to Cholly's right, sizing her up. She sauntered over to the man and jerked her head. He sat back down. Then she turned her attention to Cholly and mumbled, "Ano ang, kailaugan mo dita?"

Cholly replied in Tagalog and the woman acted as if she didn't understand her. Cholly repeated her answer, then snapped, "Answer in English; I know damn well you understand me."

The woman's face went from hostile to a forced, insincere half smile. "Who you look?"

57

"A big man, Hawaiian, tattoo on his arm. He came in here a few minutes ago," she lied.

"Thas bullshit and you know it, Chan," a cold voice shot out from the left side of the room.

Cholly unhappily recognized its owner, Man Mountain Mean. It was a nickname, but it suited the behemoth.

"Well, well, well, when did you get out, 3M?"

"You know that as well as I do, you bitch. You sent me up."

"Right, but that was a long time ago. I hope you keep your nose clean this time." As she spoke, Cholly slowly eased her way toward the back of the room. She noticed Gus leaning against the left side of the back wall. He inclined his head slightly toward the pay phone on his right.

She felt sweat under her arms and running down between her breasts. Oh. God, Kam, I need you. She put her left hand in her trouser pocket and pulled out a stick of gum. Then she put both hands behind her back and continued her stroll toward the phone. When she reached it, she eased around to lean back while still studying the room.

Everyone continued to watch her, and the silence was unnerving. She took the gum out of her mouth and slowly inched her right hand back under the shelf of the phone stand as if getting rid of it and at the same time she pulled off a tiny roll of paper. The wrinkled tissue would look like a cigarette. She tried to palm it, but her hands were slick with sweat. She pushed away from the phone and shuffled toward Gus. She put the phony cigarette in the corner of her lips, then stopped in front of him.

"What the hell you looking at, dirtbag?" She grabbed the front of his shirt, pulling him toward her. She pushed him back after she slipped the pencil-thin roll of money into his shirt pocket."

"Nuth — nuthin' — let me go, I ain't done nothin'."

She reached over, smoothed down the material she had clutched, then patted his cheek a little too hard. "See that you keep it that way."

Suddenly, Cholly realized she was in trouble. The aisle that ran between the tables was U-shaped. In order to continue toward the front door, she would have to pass the Mountain. On his best day he was deadly and unpredictable. But she couldn't retrace her steps without losing face, and bravado was all she had going for her. Subtly, she shifted her arm against her gun butt, making sure everyone saw her actions. A little bluff never hurt at a time like this.

She moved slowly. Every step was agony. All she really wanted to do was run like hell. She moved her eyes from side to side as if saying, "Behave; I'll remember you."

Finally, she was even with Mountain's table. She barely flicked an eye in his direction, but suddenly his hand shot up and a flame flickered near her face, then inched toward the rolled up piece of paper. "Light, pig?"

She pushed the hand away with, "I'm trying to quit" and moved on. She heard him suck in his breath, then curse her in Hawaiian. She ignored him and kept walking. A chair scraped across the floor.

The last thing she wanted to do was pull her gun, but she had to make a quick decision. She heard the chair move again, and then fall over. A shuffling sound was cut short with the metallic staccato of an automatic being slid back. Then a calm voice suggested, "Unless you're growing, I suggest you sit down."

All heads turned to the back of the room. Hawk was standing in front of the men's room door, a .45 leveled at Mountain's chest. He never took his eyes off the big man as Cholly covered the remaining distance to the front door.

The shift from the dark interior to the afternoon sun blinded her for a second, but then she ran around to the back to cover Hawk's exit. Deciding discretion was the better part of valor, she pulled her gun. Hawk was already out the back door and had pushed a dumpster in front of it.

"You really think that would ever stop that mountain of a man?" she asked.

"No, but the noise will give us a warning." He looked down at her and realized she wasn't as cool as she pretended to be. "You okay, Cholly?"

"Yes." Her voice quivered and he slid a comforting arm around her shoulder, pulling her to his side. She relished the feeling of safety for a hair's breadth, then lashed out in misplaced anger. "I told you to stay in the car! What the hell did you think you were doing, disobeying a direct order?"

"And you're welcome, ma'am," he spit out as he dropped his arm from around her and marched away to the car.

# Chapter 17

It was early evening before Cholly had the energy to take the note to Kam. He looked at the smeared paper and asked, "What did you have to do, eat it?"

"Almost." He could hear the weariness in her voice and reached out a comforting hand.

Before he could unwrap the roll, the door opened and Hawk entered. He noticed their hand-holding but pretended not to see it and instead introduced himself to Kam as if the other night had never happened.

Kam had no chance to return the greeting because Cholly cut in with "What are you doing, Hawkins, following me?"

"Hardly."

"Then how did you —"

"I know how you think. Besides, it figures you'd bring the note to Kam, since Gus is his snitch."

Carefully, Kam unwound the paper and smoothed it out. He studied it a second and then frowned at what he saw.

Cholly leaned over him to look, too. Hawk stayed put.

"I know Gus can't write and you've got your picture language, but I don't get it. What does it mean?" Cholly asked.

"Kam studied the two vague drawings. "Damned if I know. The bottom one's a fish but I don't know what kind. And the top thing looks like a bad drawing of a mountain."

Kam turned the sheet around so Hawk could look at it. To some degree, Kam was right. What could be a mountain had high ridges in the middle, but then they dropped away on each side. "What was Gus checking out for you?"

"That guy, Young's, background. What he had to do with the sovereignty movement. You know, da kine."

"Right. Da kine." Hawk took the paper from Kam and turned it slightly one way, then another, and finally upright again. After studying the drawings for a few moments, he remarked, "Beauty pageant."

"What?" Kam and Cholly echoed in unison.

"Beauty pageants. I mean, the crowns. That's what the top drawing looks like to me."

"What would beauty pageants have to do with murder or the sover —" Cholly didn't get to finish her sentence.

"Of course!" Hawk snapped his fingers, then looked at the drawing again. "The fish, I'll bet it's supposed to represent a herring. I think Gus is trying to tell us that the sovereignty bit is just a red herring."

"He thinks the sovereignty thing has nothing to do with the murders?" asked Kam.

"That'd be my guess," said Hawk. He and Kam exchanged satisfied looks.

"Do you mean I almost got creamed for *that*?" Cholly fumed.

Kam reached out to comfort her. It was a bit too much for Hawk.

# Chapter 18

Hawk tore out of the hospital like it was on fire. He couldn't, or wouldn't look at why the intimacy between Kam and Cholly bothered him. He stomped up the sidewalk, then stopped beside his car as if he had run out of steam.

"What's with you, Hawkins? Why can't you spend five minutes with that woman without losing it?" He leaned his arms on the roof of the car and took several deep breaths.

The early evening air was heavy with the perfume from rose bushes that surrounded several nearby golden shower trees. Their yellow blossoms spread out, making the trees look like giant umbrellas. Hawk concentrated on the beauty of his surroundings, trying to get back to normal. A glance westward told him there was going to be another beautiful sunset.

Suddenly, an overwhelming sense of loneliness engulfed him. He had come to Hawaii to start a new life, but obviously he had brought all his emotional baggage with him. And the only people he had spent time with so far were drug dealers, gang members and murderers. If Hawk had thought he would find friends in his new division or with his new partner, he had been sadly mistaken. No one was actually unfriendly, except for the Dragon Lady, but he still felt like a kid standing outside the candy shop window looking in.

He slapped the roof of the car in a burst of impatience with himself, then wrenched open the door. "If you want to punch out something, why not go to the gym?" He didn't turn around at the sound of the familiar voice. He was off duty; he could ignore her.

Hawk got into his car and pulled out of the parking lot and on to Punchbowl. Maybe he could find a spot to watch the sunset and improve his mood. He drove only a few blocks before he saw the flashing lights of a patrol car in his rearview mirror. Cholly had a grim look on her face as she motioned him over.

When she came up to the window on the driver's side, he gave her a sarcastic, "Do you want to see my driver's license, officer?"

"What I want to see, Hawkins, is you lighten up. Follow me."

"I'm off duty; you can go to …" but she was already back in her car. To ignore her would make him feel even more childish than he suddenly felt. He followed her down to Ala Moana and turned right behind her. He was surprised when she turned left into the street that ran along Pier Seven.

Several tour buses were unloading passengers for a dinner cruise. Cholly pulled up into the circular drive in front of the Maritime Museum and motioned for Hawk to give his car to the valet parking attendant. She drove back out and parked on the street, then joined him.

"Well, ma'am, may I ask what we are doing here?"

"Having dinner, and hopefully a spectacular sunset." She moved along the side of the building toward a restaurant on the waterfront. "Have you been on the Falls of Clyde yet?" She motioned to the four-masted schooner anchored a few feet away.

"No."

"It's really special; it's something you ought to make time to see."

"Coming from Boston —" he didn't really mean to make his remark sound like a put down, but that's the way it came out.

"Oh, yeah, I forgot." She stopped and turned toward him, a look of indecision on her face. "You know, maybe this wasn't such a good idea after all. I thought you looked a little down, that maybe if we had a peaceful meal in a pleasant atmosphere, it might cheer you up. I guess I was wrong, so if you want to run along --"

"Mea culpa, Lieutenant. I'm the one who should apologize." He took her arm and headed toward the water. "Let's start over again, okay?" She nodded, but there was a look of reservation in her eyes.

They were having a pre-dinner drink when Cholly grabbed his forearm and ordered, "Look quickly or you'll miss it." She had fixed her gaze on the sun, which was disappearing behind the horizon in a blaze of glory. Before Hawk could ask her what he was looking for, a flash of green encircled the rim of the setting sun. He blinked, as if doubting what he saw, and then it was gone.

"Beautiful, isn't it?" Cholly was like a breathless child staring at a wonder of the world. "I always get 'chicken skin' when I see that."

"That is an incredible sight, something I've never seen before." He paused and took a sip of his drink, a thoughtful frown on his face. "Now, let me guess, 'chicken skin' ... of course, goose bumps!"

"You're a good student after all. I'm glad you got to see that sunset. It doesn't happen all the time; conditions have to be just right." Her face was flushed, her eyes shining. She continued to stare at the horizon, even though the sun had sunk below the waterline.

"You act as if it was the first time you ever saw it."

"I can never get enough of all of this," she said as her fingers swept a graceful arch that included the waterfront and park across the bay. "We have an expression, 'Lucky we live Hawaii' and there's hardly a day of my life that I don't think that."

Cholly had ordered opah and encouraged Hawk to try it. He attacked the moonfish like he hadn't eaten for a week. An atmosphere of calm settled over them, allowing Cholly's basically friendly nature to seep out.

"Tell me the truth, Hawkins the Third, why did you decide to come to Hawaii?"

Hawk paused, a forkful of baked potato stopped in midair. He felt as if he had reached a crossroads. His first inclination was to tell her to mind her own business, but if he really was going to stay here and build a new life, then he had to loosen up a bit with the locals.

"Two months ago, my fiancée broke our engagement. Or maybe I should say she put it on hold."

"Oh hold?"

"Until I come to my senses, to quote her ultimatum."

"Let me guess — she doesn't like the idea of being married to a cop?"

"You clairvoyant?"

67

"Nope, it's an occupational hazard. That's why I'm not getting married."

"Never?"

"Maybe in five or six years; maybe not." Her voice was flat, emotionless.

"You don't want a home ... a family?" Cholly heard a wistful tone in the question, but Hawk's face was bland looking as he continued eating.

"I've got family coming out of my ears. And I have a home. It's all mine, no one to cater to, to ask permission of or to pick up after."

"And no one to cuddle up with on a cold winter night."

"Oh, yeah, I really miss that in *this* climate, Number Three."

Hawk noticed a certain air of defensiveness in her reply.

They finished their meal in relative silence, each deeply lost in private thoughts. But their mood lightened with dessert and coffee.

"You were right, this lemon mousse is excellent. But what I don't understand, Chan, is how you keep your figure. You eat as much as a man."

"Metabolism and aerobics class ... ugh, there should be a law against exercise." She all but licked the parfait glass clean, then eyed Hawk's half-eaten helping.

With a smile, he slid the dessert plate in front of her. "Be my guest."

"Mahalo, you all." She dug in as if she were starving, not noticing that he sat with his chin resting on his folded hands, watching her every move. She ran her tongue around the edge of her lips to be sure she hadn't missed a drop. When she caught a strange look in Hawk's eyes, she demanded, "What?"

"Who might be a better question. You're like a kid at Christmas. If I had known that all it would take to soften you up was a good meal, I'd have taken you out before."

"I'm taking you, remember. And I don't want to be softened up."

"Why not?"

"That's a good way to get killed."

"Oh, come on now, you don't really believe that."

"Like hell I don't. Between fighting the scumbags and proving I'm as good as any man, soft doesn't cut it.

Hawk reached out and covered her hand with his. Cholly didn't realize she had become chilled until his palm warmed her. "Are you afraid to let yourself be just a woman, a human being?" he asked.

The conversation was taking a turn she preferred to avoid. Normally, she discouraged this line of conversation, but as with everything else that was connected with Alexander Woodrow Hawkins III, things didn't always turn out the way she expected.

# Chapter 19

The next morning, Cholly and Hawk reported back to Captain Kahana at police headquarters. "Well, what did you get from Rose's?" he asked.

"It wasn't worth the time," replied Cholly.

"Then you sure won't be happy with this. The lab called; the note next to Winslow's body was clean. Nothing to go on unless you find the typewriter for a match," said the Captain. He paused. "And that's the good news."

"And the rest?" asked Cholly.

"Remember the black paint chips Doc found under Young's nails? They don't match the trim at Iolani Palace. It's all brown and ivory," he stated.

Hawk interrupted. "I thought the report said there was no attempted break-in."

Cholly answered him, "We didn't find any signs of it, but he did have those pieces and we don't know where they came from." Noticing that Hawk was no longer paying attention to her, she turned back to the Captain.

"We still can't find any connection between the two victims," she said thoughtfully, "and though it looks like they both belonged to the sovereignty movement, our snitch says that's a red herring. We need to look a little more into Hiram, he may be into some Mah Jongg gambling."

"So what have you got for sure?" asked the Captain.

"We're working on it," was Cholly's reply.

"Well how about some wiki wiki, Chan. Murder is bad for the tourist trade," he scolded.

"I guess it's time we tried the big grapevine. Prepare yourself for a treat, Number Three, tomorrow you get to meet Toady," Cholly said, nudging Hawk to get his attention.

Pulled back from his thoughts, Hawk suggested, "Try this on for size. According to the file on our first victim, his wife has a compulsion to steal. What if her husband wasn't taking the cup; instead he was trying to put it back?"

# Chapter 20

As Cholly and Hawk drove along the coast of the north shore, he savored the scenery. The cloudless cobalt blue swooped down to meet the horizon; the water looked like silver-flecked charcoal where the sun reflected its rays. Despite growing up on an ocean-front estate, Hawk was still fascinated by the vivid combinations of the colors the tropical waters made.

"Beautiful, isn't it?" Cholly asked.

"I've seen beaches all over the world, but nothing's any prettier than this. I hope you appreciate what you have here."

"Oh, I do. I don't know how people can live anywhere else. Sometimes I think the ocean is my mana, where my power comes from."

"I heard it was the land that had life; maybe even the rocks, trees — "

"We Hawaiians believe everything has the breath of life in it. No matter how bummed out I get, if I can just crash on the shoreline, things look a lot better real fast." Cholly turned off the paved highway onto a red dirt road. "Okay, here we go; Toady's place is dead ahead."

A path had been cut through the cane fields, allowing the trucks to come in to gather the tall sugar cane stalks. Hawk swiveled his head to watch the gracefully swaying stalks that towered over the roof of their car. Red dust swirled behind the car as they crested a hill.

Hawk took a deep breath as they again saw the ocean, but this time from several miles away. The blue waves were fringed with frothy white as they slapped against the shore. The peaceful scene was suddenly disturbed when a burley man with an assault rifle moved onto the road in front of them and blocked their way.

Hawk's hand moved toward his holster but Cholly ordered, "Leave it!"

"Aloha, Billy J. When did you get out?"

"You should know damn well, since you sent me up. What you doin' here?" Without waiting for an answer, he stepped closer to the squad car and peered in the window at Hawk. "Where's your better half?"

"In the hospital."

A joyous roar escaped the otherwise pinched lips. "All right! One down, one to go!"

"You should live so long. And lose the hardware unless you want to go back to O triple C."

"Hey, Chan, I did my time. Remember the Constitution. I got a right to bear arms — "

"The only rights you got, scumbag, are the ones I give you."

"But this is part of my job. I'm a security consultant."

Cholly's sarcastic snort would have cut through steel. Since her next comment was in Hawaiian, Hawk could only guess at what she said before lapsing back into English. "Don't go even one inch off the reservation with that thing and keep your nose clean, if that's possible. Now tell the man I'm coming in," she said as she hit the accelerator.

They continued down the road through the cane stalks for a few more minutes, then moved off to an overgrown driveway that led onto a large circular clearing. At the back of the open space was a decrepit shack sitting on plantation-style stilts. A wide lanai encircled the house. The rusted corrugated roof was partially covered with the dried brown needles of the Norfolk pine tree that shaded it.

Cholly scrunched the car to a stop on the gravel area in front of the worn wooden steps. Hawk stiffened, his eyes scanning the scene, which included a worn tin sign hanging from one nail. In rust-splattered letters it proclaimed, "Café." Cholly could sense his hesitation.

Hawk ran his tongue around suddenly dry lips. It wasn't easy to keep his hand away from his weapon, but nuts as she appeared to be, instinct told him he could trust Cholly's judgement.

As if she could read his thoughts, she remarked, "Trust me, Hawkins, I don't have a death wish. I've been through this drill before. Just keep your gun holstered and your mouth shut. No matter what goes down, just play dumb."

Coming in from the bright sunlight, it was difficult for them to see anything. The café's interior was shrouded in darkness. Hawk sensed the presence of movement behind them but kept his face impassive. Cholly slipped in front of him, knocked a pile of dirty towels off a high stool next to the counter, then perched on the edge of the seat.

"With all your money, I'd think you could at least get someone to come in and clean up this pigsty."

"You got lots o' guts, Chan. You know better than to drop in on me. Next time you call first, then mebbe I get fix up for you … that is, if there is a 'next time.'"

The last words were in a tone just this side of a threat. Hawk's eyes had adjusted to the gloom and now he had to bite his lip to keep a straight face.

Sprawled on what looked like a daybed made out of woven leaves, was the largest man he had seen this side of a Sumo wrestler; he weighed at least 450 pounds! What looked like slim Sumo wrestlers stood guard at the head and foot of the bed.

"Okay, now that we have the chit chat done with, how 'bout something to eat? Then we'll talk story." Cholly slid off the stool and took a small step toward the daybed.

"The cook's sick today and I don' know no history, Chan."

"This is new history, Toady. Talk to me about the Ohana groups — and the guy who was found dead at the Palace."

"I'm not into dat sovereignty da kine."

"Maybe not, but you know everything that goes down on this island."

Toady snorted, "Go to hell, Cholly."

In a blur of blue, Cholly moved and had her gun pressed up against the bottom of his nose. With her other hand, she motioned the advancing guards to stay put.

"I probably will, but you won't be the one to send me there, *cousin*. Now, you even blink, and we'll have another funeral in the family."

Sweat beaded up on Toady's forehead, but he tried to stare her down in an attempt at bravado. "Why for you always so hu'hu? And why you give damn for dat guy?"

"It's my job." Then her voice turned to a menacing whisper. "Toady, quit stalling."

Cautiously he raised a sausage-sized finger and slowly touched the muzzle of Cholly's gun. Gently, he turned it a fraction of an inch away from his nose. "You and that damned hair trigger — some day you gonna hurt the wrong person."

Cholly backed off a few inches but said nothing, just continued staring at him.

"Okay, but I don' know nothin' 'bout them." The muzzle waved back toward him threateningly.

"I don't like dead bodies on my beat. Now tell me what you know."

With a small sigh, Toady said, "Not much. First guy's nobody. Winslow was a loud mouth."

"Who were his enemies?"

"Himself. Thought he was a big shot. Promised some land to the Ohana movement but nobody ever saw any."

"What about the cups?"

Toady laughed. "Ain't worth nothin' 'cept maybe to take a leak in."

"Then why off them?"

"Maybe da schmucks was in the wrong place at the wrong time."

"If you're lying to me ...."

"You ain't worth the effort, Loo-ten-ent."

After exchanging looks of pure venom, Cholly slid backward off the bed. "Give Aunty my aloha." With a look of contempt, she turned her back on him and sauntered out of the room.

Hawk decided to back out behind her.

At the car, Hawk noticed sweat marks between her shoulder blades. Well, well, maybe she was human after all, he mused.

"Was that little bit of grandstanding for my benefit?"

"Put a sock in it, Hawkins."

"Is that gun routine your normal style?"

"It is with pigs like him."

"Why?"

"Because otherwise he'd eat me for breakfast."

"But he knows you're bluffing."

"Like hell I am."

Cholly's nerves were wound up like a coiled spring and she sure wasn't in the mood for some smart-mouth malihini trying to give her a hard time. She started the car and gunned the accelerator. The car shot out of the clearing, spewing a thick cloud of red dirt behind it. Batting away the dust filtering in through the open windows, she turned and glared at Hawk.

"I have to treat him like that."

"Why?"

"Because he'd like to kill me."

"And what's stopping him?"

"The family."

"Wait … you really are cousins?"

"'You can chose your friends but not your relatives.' I'll give you that one gift wrapped."

"In what," Hawk snorted. "A tent?"

With a grim set to her mouth, Cholly headed the car for the highway.

# Chapter 21

The killer smiled in satisfaction. Everything was just wonderful, what with the newspapers and TV now speculating that there might be a serial killer loose in Honolulu. Reporters had tied in the fact that both men seemed to be involved in the sovereignty movement. And there was a piece of the Missionary Collection found near each of the bodies. What a stroke of genius it was to steal one from the Palace.

A gleeful laugh echoed through the deserted house. Shadows from the large banyan tree clothed it in darkness, but nothing could match the smoldering darkness in the killer's heart, which was briefly lit by a bright gleam of success. Glancing at the TV, the killer chuckled. "So they still think it is a serial killing. Good; I succeeded, and why not. After you've killed once, it becomes so much easier."

Reaching to turn off the set, a familiar face flashed on the screen: Abigail Wilson Bingham, a dried-up old spinster who looked like she had just stepped off the boat with the "First Company" of missionaries. A bitch through and through, Abigail always acted as if she were better than anyone else, being related to the last king.

The killer smiled at the patrician face pontificating on the newscast and then an idea entered the killer's brain.

"What if … uh huh … now, if I can just find a way to get another piece from the Missionary Collection ….

"This time, I'll try something else. I really hate guns. Yes, what I think Miss Abigail needs is a nice cup of tea, with a very special flavor. I don't know, oleander is so common, let's see what else I can think of. Hmm, cyanide … no that's too vulgar for such a distinguished lady. And arsenic is rather common, too. Oh, I guess we'll just stick with a lovely brew of oleander. It's more genteel, like Miss Abigail herself.

"Now that is settled, the next problem is where to kill her? If I am going to make it look like it's connected to the sovereignty movement, it needs to be a historical place. Oh, of course, Queen Emma's Summer Palace."

---

Cholly was running late. Kam was being dismissed from the hospital and she told him she'd pick him up. She didn't want to keep him waiting, but every time she had tried to leave work, the phone had rung. Now her tires screeched as she pulled up into the curved driveway near the dismissal area and raced to his room.

"Sorry to be late —" she burst through the door, then stopped, surprised to find Leilani there.

The younger woman blushed and stammered, "I thought maybe you could use some help getting him home."

"Um, sure, I guess so." Her eyes sought out Kam's, but he was watching Leilani gather up all the gifts he had received while he was a patient. The girl was the quintessential Island beauty. Silky black hair hung down to her waist and she had a figure that belonged in a health spa ad. Her beautiful skin was the color of honey and she had a sweet personality to match.

An unidentifiable pang crept through Cholly. It was clear that Leilani was in love with Kam. And from the way his eyes followed her around the room, the big guy was returning the interest.

Cholly started banging drawers, getting Kam's belongings packed.

"Hey, Ipo, what's the matter with you?"

Cholly ignored him and continued packing. Kam looked at Leilani, who sensed a problem and decided she needed to go buy something in the gift shop.

"Save the furniture or I'll get billed for it," he cracked, trying to get Cholly's attention.

Cholly stopped, took a deep breath and finished at a normal pace. "I'm sorry."

"What's bugging you besides your new partner?"

"Nothing."

"Hey, kid, it's me. Since when you lie to your best friend?" He paused, then added, "Is it Leilani?"

"No!" the word burst out. "Yes."

"But no, she's your friend; she even told me you said to come."

"I know." Cholly threw her hands up in surrender and plopped down on the bed next to him. "I don't know what's the matter with me these days, Ipo. I should be happy for you, that you're starting to live again, but …."

"Maybe it's hard to be happy for someone else when you're miserable."

"But I'm not. I have everything I want, except you riding shotgun with me. But that'll change pretty soon. Doc says he never saw anyone heal as quickly as you."

81

"We're not talking about me. It's your happiness I'm worried about"

"You one pupule kanaka. There's nothing wrong with my life."

Kam said nothing, but just quietly shook his head.

# Chapter 22

Hawk arrived at the office early and was typing a report when the Captain came in. "Hiya, Hawk, are you busy Sunday?"

"I'm playing tennis in the morning."

"But after that you free?"

"Yes, what do you need?"

"Nothing. I want to take you to a wedding, that's all."

"A wedding. What would the bride and groom think about you bringing a stranger to the wedding?"

"You in the Islands, boy. All time we bring friends; everyone have fun, b-i-g luau. My niece, my sister no care, always welcome everyone."

Hawk was flattered and smiled his thanks. "Where is it and what time?"

"One o'clock at Kahaiwahoa Church. But I'll have one of my kids pick you up. You'll get lost getting to the luau; it's up on the north shore."

"Thanks; I mean mahalo, Captain." The Captain waved off the thanks and moved into his office as Cholly came around the corner.

"What are you thanking him for?"

"He invited me to a wedding Sunday."

Cholly wondered to herself, Pualani's wedding? She turned and frowned at the closed door. Why in the world would he do that? Hawk would really be a fish out of water.

She could admit that he was trying to adapt to Island life, but she couldn't see him with the uninhibited bunch that would be at the wedding and luau.

Although she made no comment, Hawk picked up on her displeasure, which made him wonder why she would mind if he went to a wedding with the captain unless ....

"Are you going to be there?"

"Sure, she's my cousin."

"For real, or calabash?"

"Very good, the Third. You're catching on. For real."

"Is everyone on this island related to everyone else?"

"Just about, if you count calabash. You have to remember there aren't that many Hawaiians left and a lot of us live on Oahu."

"From some of your conversations, I figured you thought of yourself as Chinese."

"No, I feel more Hawaiian, even though my parents lean toward the Chinese side. There's a certain — mystique — for want of a better word. If you're here long enough, and open your mind, you'll see what I mean.

"What should I wear?"

"Believe it or not, a suit to the church. Pua is having a formal wedding. But bring along stuff to change into. I know we'll have a volleyball game and some of us will go swimming eventually."

# Chapter 23

Hawk felt very much at home in the old church. In many ways, it reminded him of some of the churches in New England. There was a certain sense of tranquility and stability in the white walls and the dark woods.

And it was a perfect backdrop for the riot of colors in the guest's clothes. The formal attire for the bridal party consisted of pearl-gray tuxedos for the men and pastel floral for the bridesmaids, but the friends and family had chosen every color of the rainbow. The flowers reflected a wide selection of the local varieties — from orchids to anthurium and gardenias to roses.

Hawk was seated on the aisle and there was a beribboned bouquet next to his shoulder. The tuberose fragrance was almost overpowering and he was certain he would never forget the aroma.

The Kahana boy who picked him up showed him where his dad was sitting, then left him with, "Later, dude," and took off to sit with his buddies.

While waiting for the ceremony to start, Hawk was introduced to a rotund, jovial Rosy Kahana. And an elderly lady next to her was simply "Aunty Irma." With almost snow-white hair contrasting against her mellow brown skin, she was the epitome of patrician beauty and elegance.

Hawk found the mixture of people fascinating. But as his gaze swept the congregation, he realized one face was missing.

"She's going to be late," the Captain remarked, reading Hawk's mind.

"Who?" Hawk feigned ignorance, but his boss gave him a wry grin and did not answer.

"She still keeping you hu'hu?"

"On the bad days. That woman sure knows how to get to you, doesn't she?"

"Yeah, it's the Chinese in her. Wish she was more Scottish, like Aunty," he said as he nodded in the direction of the older lady. "She's sweet like fresh cane right from the field."

Hawk raised his eyebrows in question and the Captain remarked, "That's one of Cholly's great grandmothers, a Tutu."

At that moment, Hawk noticed a movement at a side door near the altar. A strikingly handsome couple had entered and were moving down the side aisle toward the middle of the church. At first, he almost didn't recognize his partner.

Her hair, which was always up in what his grandmother called a "washer-woman knot" hung loose down past her shoulders. She was wearing a yellow and white print dress. The bodice was softly draped in diagonal folds which created a deep vee. The skirt hugged her hips, then flared out at the knees. Though Hawk couldn't see the rest of her, instinct told him her legs would go on forever.

He found himself being squished up against the pew as the family moved over for Cholly and her escort. The Captain smiled an apology. "That Greg, he takes up a lot of room. He plays for the Dallas Cowboys."

Hawk mumbled, "I can believe it," as he watched them move toward their seats. On the matter of the legs, he was right. White slingbacks arched onto the most graceful legs he had seen in a long time. For a second, he had to mentally shake himself. There was no doubt she was a woman, the way she filled out her uniform. But *this* was one beautiful, very feminine lady.

Greg remained standing a second to answer someone talking to him from the row ahead of them. Hawk hated to admit it, even to himself, but he was one of the most handsome men he had ever seen. He was big in the manner Hawk had come to recognize as a Polynesian way. But his features were defined in a more "haole" way, so he must be "chop suey." As the man turned to his seat, he gave Cholly a smile that would have defrosted the Himalayas. Hawk felt a strange surge of emotion sweep through him. If he hadn't known better, he would have sworn it was jealousy.

The ceremony was in both Hawaiian and English, as was the music. Hawk found it soothing enough to feel almost ethereal. He had heard the "Hawaiian Wedding Song" before and never found it particularly appealing, but today it sounded just perfect. He felt almost transported to some peaceful, secret place. He wasn't even aware of the fact the guests were ready to leave until the Captain put a hand on his shoulder. "Are you all right?"

Hawk was a bit flustered, but stammered, "Sure. I just, well, I guess I got caught up in the ceremony."

"It was beautiful, wasn't it." Rosy beamed. "I'm glad you liked it. Kimo says you are trying hard to appreciate our customs."

"Yes, ma'am, but I must admit I get confused."

She gave a chuckle that seemed to start at her toes. "As do we sometimes."

They exited the church and Hawk caught sight of Cholly's backside swishing along beside her hunk of a date. He didn't know what their relationship was, but she looked hot enough to sizzle.

Hawk rode to the luau with the Captain and Rosy. When they got to the house, he retrieved his clothes from the son's car and changed into a pair of white shorts and a blue and green aloha shirt. By the time Rosy had introduced him to a dozen or so people, he started to feel right at home.

Tables had been set up along one side of the house, under a large banyan tree. As Hawk glanced over the repast, he realized it gave a new meaning to the word "groaning board." He thought his grandmother's Christmas dinners were elaborate, but this almost eclipsed them.

Whole salmons rested in nests of greens decorated with lemon slices. Sea shells almost two feet across held a variety of food from potato salad and macaroni salad to an Island staple, Jello with white, red and green bands. There was even a bowl of lomilomi, the raw salmon that was "massaged" with oil and spices, another traditional dish.

Large wooden platters which Hawk recognized as koa wood were filled with beautiful arrangements of papaya, mangos and bananas centered around pineapples that had been interlaced with slices of bright green kiwi.

The opaque whiteness of haupia seemed bland by comparison, but Hawk had already become a devotee of the coconut pudding and knew it tasted better than it looked.

Everything was ready except the pig. As the last guests arrived, the men went over to the imu, an earthen oven that was covered with wet burlap and palm leaves. A great ceremony was made of removing the pig, then taking the hot stones out of the cavity and sliding a sturdy pole through the carcass so that it could be carried to the carving table.

The older boys carefully gathered the sweet potatoes that had been baked in the imu and added them to the feast. The aroma of the meat made Hawk's mouth water. Cholly had introduced him to this delicacy one day at lunchtime. More than one dinner had been a takeout meal of this Polynesian treat.

People formed several lines, then moved on to sit on lau hala mats that had been set around the grounds. Hawk's brief introduction to the old native craft had been when he saw the entrance hall rug Cholly was making. He was impressed with the effort it took to make these and stood almost speechless at the room-sized beauties in front of him.

"Sometimes a whole village will work on those large ones," a voice commented from behind him.

He turned to find a fresh version of his partner standing there. She was barefoot and dressed in a gauzy pink flowered pareau. A white hibiscus held the hair away from the right side of her face. She wore a white lei whose perfume wove a net around him. Hawk looked down at her scrubbed fresh face and shining eyes and had to fight to keep from kissing her.

"What's the matter, Number Three? You look funny."

"I — uh — ." His lips were suddenly dry, his throat felt too parched to speak. "I was just trying to figure out what *that* flower was." He pointed at her lei just as someone pushed against her and she leaned against his finger. His other fingers brushed against the top of her breast and he pulled back as if he had touched fire.

"It's white ginger. Here, smell. Although she lifted the lei up toward his nose, he still had to lean down, and again the desire to take her in his arms was overwhelming.

Despite the delicious meal, Hawk was miserable during dinner. Cholly sat next to him, with Greg on her other side. Though she tried to include Hawk in the conversation, the other man seemed determined to monopolize her. After answering a question she had asked him, Hawk mentioned this. Cholly commented, "I'm sorry, I don't mean to ignore you, but Greg doesn't get to town very often; we don't get to spend much time together."

She turned and gave Greg a wistful look. In response, he put a ham-sized hand around her shoulder and pulled her closer for a chaste kiss on the cheek. Hawk's imagination suddenly ran wild and he had no trouble visualizing something more intimate later on.

Hawk almost glared at the man, but when he asked if something was the matter, Hawk just said, "You look familiar but I know we haven't met before."

"Maybe I look like someone you arrested, yeah?" The football player laughed a little too forcefully at his own joke.

"He's Kam's brother; they look enough alike to be twins."

Hawk could only force out a weak, "Oh," and went back to trying to make the delicious food go down his still-dry throat.

The meal went on for hours, interspersed with a band playing, or various guests getting up to play the ukulele or guitars. Part of Hawk was having a good time, the other part wished he had driven his own car so he could leave.

Moving away from the festivities, he went to stand along the seawall and stare out at the ocean. The normally soothing sound of the waves lapping at the wall did not help his mood. He fought trying to look at what was causing this moroseness, but eventually it seemed easier to face the problem than avoid it.

He didn't know when it had happened, but he had gone from almost detesting Cholly to wanting her. It made no sense to him. The woman had made a point of making his life miserable, to ridicule him and everything his lifestyle stood for, yet she filled his thoughts day and night lately.

Cholly watched Hawk move toward the seawall. His shoulders sagged; he seemed listless. She had known he wouldn't have a good time here and felt sorry for him. Although she did give him credit for trying to adjust, and acknowledged to herself that he had done a pretty good job of it, still the fact remained that this atmosphere was too radical a change for a Boston Brahmin.

Some of the men who had been enjoying the okole all afternoon decided to do the hula between the band's numbers. Hawk heard the strains of the music and laughter and wandered back to investigate.

The three men were outstanding dancers. Hawk was surprised, and remarked about that to the Captain.

"The first hula dancers were men. Some of the best kuma hulas, teachers, are men. If you can get a ticket, you should go over to Hilo for the Merry Monarch Festival. Then you see really primo hula." With that, the Captain went to join the dancers.

For a man his size, he was very graceful. Hawk soon lost himself to the music and the gestures.

"Want me to translate for you, Hawkins?" Cholly was standing next to him.

"Translate what? No one's singing."

"The movements ... each one means something. There, that's a mountain, and now the fingers are the rain coming down onto the mountain. The fingers brushing the lips then extending toward you usually mean 'I like or love you,' or they can also mean 'a kiss.'"

She leaned in front of him a bit in order to get a better view of the performers. She hesitated to translate some of the movements, but they were so suggestive, Hawk didn't need any words to understand them. He meant to lightly tease her, "Since when does anything embarrass the fastest mouth in the Pacific?" came out brusquely, but he was fighting a plethora of emotions, all of which were focused on the delectable body in front of him.

Cholly turned and looked at him. His breathing was shallow and he had a look on his face that she couldn't interpret. A current of charged sexuality ran between them. She shivered and moved away.

Another magnificent sunset, complete with the rare flash of green, came as the sun plunged into the sea. Some of the families with small children had left, but most of the guests were still enjoying the festivities. Many of the older folks sang songs, then did their own version of the hula. Repeatedly, Hawk reveled in the graceful movements, the

93

subtle sensuality that seemed to fill the flower-scented night breezes.

Yet at the same time, a sense of loneliness almost overwhelmed him. He might have gotten his fiancée, Allyson, out of his life, but he was no closer to fulfilling his dreams than he had been before. And it hurt to admit it, but more and more he seemed to find himself thinking of his partner.

He realized that he had managed to jump from the proverbial frying pan into a fire that would smother him if he wasn't careful.

Hawk was too restless to stay any longer. He decided to see if he could find anyone who would be leaving soon. As he turned back to face the dance area, the pahua, or drums, started again and a gasp of pleasure went up from the guests. He moved closer and his heart skipped two beats.

Cholly and a young man he didn't recognize were performing what he knew had to be a courtship or mating dance. Though it was doing things to his body that he wished he could control, he couldn't force himself to leave.

Both dancers were so languidly graceful that it was as if neither of them had a backbone. As the music increased in tempo, the steps became frenzied; the dancers' bodies glistened in the light of the large fire between the band and the dancers.

The dance ended with thunderous applause. Unconsciously, Hawk moved toward a circle of guests and sat down on the ground. The young man moved over to his friends, but as the music began again, Cholly started to dance a solo.

A hush fell over the crowd; they watched, almost hypnotized, as the lithe body seemed to float through the night air. Hawk could not catch his breath. He had never noticed how long and graceful her fingers were; now they were sketching out every loving gesture she had translated earlier, and quite a few more.

As the tempo of the music increased, Cholly moved to stand directly in front of Hawk, obviously dedicating the dance to him. Under other circumstances he might have been embarrassed, but he was too mesmerized by the undulating body beckoning to him.

When she reached out to place a feather-light stroke along his cheek, he tried to grab her hand, but she eluded him with a laugh and a nimble side step.

Finally, the dance came to an end, and Cholly collapsed in the center of the circle to thunderous applause. She finally looked up, gazed at Hawk for a microsecond, then ran off toward the wooded area next to the beach.

Oblivious to the remarks floating around him, Hawk took off after her, forgetting any sense of propriety. As he dodged through the underbrush, he realized that he was behaving like a horny teenager — but he didn't care.

He followed the sounds she made as she cut a path through the trees, then slowed down as he realized he could no longer hear her. He turned left and made his way down to the beach. As he emerged and looked around, Hawk was surprised to see how far away the lights of the party were. He turned the other way and started running along the shore.

He could not see Cholly, but as he moved further down the beach, he saw her pareau lying on a piece of driftwood. Turning to the water, he caught a flash of movement skimming along the moonlit surface. Without hesitation, he pulled off his clothes and ran into the water.

Cholly could not calm down. Her breathing was still irregular, her heartbeat was so strong she wondered if it could break a rib. Her face burned with humiliation. How could she have done that dance for Hawk? She had literally thrown herself at him. Thank heavens he didn't know what it meant, but everyone else did. She'd never live it down.

She was so absorbed in her thoughts that she didn't realize she was not alone until she felt a tug at her ankle. Caution and fear fought panic; there couldn't be a shark in this bay —. Hawk broke the surface with a grim, but she was ready to chew his head off.

"Of all the damn stupid things to do — don't you know we have sharks around here, you — you!" She didn't have time to finish as he pulled her to him with one arm and covered her protesting mouth with his.

Cool water was supposed to dampen one's ardor, but it wasn't working in this case. They came together like a magnet to metal. The kiss dragged on, Hawk treading water and holding them both up. Finally they started to sink and they broke away to swim toward shore. But as soon as Hawk could stand, he pulled her to him and renewed his pleasant assault.

Cholly reveled in the feel of his hard chest against her naked flesh. She squirmed against his nakedness and he groaned. "Did you know what you were starting when you did that version of the hula?"

"I — I'm not sure — ." His hand moved to caress her, and she moaned with desire. "Oh, Hawk, I ... please ...." Her words were lost as she sought and claimed his mouth. She barely realized that while still kissing her, he swung her up into his arms and moved toward the shore.

An outcropping of trees formed a small cove, the damp sand there barely touched by the waves. Hawk lowered Cholly to her feet, then pulled her against him again. She moved closer in a gesture of passionate surrender.

As they sank to the sand, she thought she'd die of longing. And when he covered her trembling body with his, she realized that she had been waiting for him all of her life.

Time stood still, then flew by. Words of love, endearments that sounded of permanence floated through the soft breeze. The frustration of a sexual tension that neither had been willing to admit to evaporated in the arms of love and passion and caring.

When Hawk whispered, "I've been looking for you all of my life," Cholly started to cry. Her heart was so full of love for him, she thought it would burst. And he — wonder of wonders — returned that love.

A curtain of black hair swirled around him as she leaned over to place another kiss on his beloved face. As she straightened up, a flash in the sky caught their eyes. "Hm, a shooting star; that just confirms what a lucky night this is, darling."

He pulled her down for another kiss, but Cholly didn't rejoice in the so-called luck. Maybe her amukua was sending her a different message.

# Chapter 24

Hawk leaned his 6′ 2″ frame against the wall outside of Cholly's gate. He was worried about his reception. Last night she hadn't uttered a word as she drove them back from the beach. She simply dropped him off at his apartment and sped away into the night.

He wiped the back of his hand across a damp brow. It wasn't the heat of the tropical morning that bothered him, but dread of what the "fastest mouth in paradise" might say.

As Hawk reached for the doorbell, he reminded himself, "You waited 10 years to fall in love. And knowing that chili pepper, she'll probably have your guts for breakfast."

Lt. Kaloke Chan had some problems, not the least of which was getting her long hair twisted up into a top knot. Looking into the mirror, she half smiled at her reflection. She wondered what the reaction would be when everyone saw her out of uniform for the first time. Somehow, it seemed time for a change.

Looking at her reflection in a skirt and white blouse, she saw beyond them and her fumbling fingers to the heart of the matter. Tears filled eyes that ached from lack of sleep.

For a second she felt light-headed. Her hands gripped the edge of the sink, knuckles turning white under her tan. Why, oh why had she danced that seductive hula for Hawk? When they weren't bickering, they were out-and-out fighting. And he would probably be going back to the mainland when their case was solved, anyway.

Through the years, Cholly had more offers than there was sand on the beach. She had just never met the right man before. Was Sergeant Alexander Woodrow Hawkins III the right man for her?

The sound of the bell pulled her back to reality. After wiping her sweaty palms against her denim skirt, she moved to open the door for her enemy. Cholly was certain that Hawk would be smug or sarcastic. But instead, the face that greeted her was filled with unabashed love.

He hoped to make points by greeting her in Hawaiian. "Aloha, kakahiaka, my love." His hand reached out toward her, but she retreated toward the house and snapped at him.

"You're wrong on both accounts, Sergeant. It is neither a good morning, nor am I your love."

Hawk hadn't really expected her to fall into his arms with the same unbridled passion she had exhibited last night, but he was a bit overwhelmed by being greeted with such raw fury. He breathed a sigh of frustration. There were probably 50 million women in the country — why did he have to fall in love with "Hell on Wheels?"

"Honey, we have to talk. I know you probably feel embarrassed —" at her raised eyebrow, he amended his remark to "uncomfortable about last night, but you shouldn't be. Something wonderful happened between us. I know that maybe I'm rushing things ...."

"Okay, Sergeant, let's clear the air. First, there is no 'us.' Last night was just one of those things. Face it, we were at a very uninhibited luau — probably drank too much okolehao — and ended up on a secluded beach. Throw in the moonlight and soft whisper of the waves and you have

99

a very seductive setup." Was it her imagination, or were they both breathing a little faster?

She scolded herself. "Keep it up, Chan, and you'll end up telling him how much you love him."

"Oh, Cholly, we both know it was more than that."

"The only thing I know, Hawkins, is we have a couple of homicides to solve."

She grabbed her purse, then stood looking with dismay at her holster and gun. Though agitated and very upset, a smile flickered over Hawk's face: he realized she'd never been out of uniform before. "How come you decided to lose the uniform now?"

She ignored his question and gave him a look so dark, it could have caused a blackout on the whole island.

"Why don't you just put it in your purse, like everyone else does?"

Silently she nodded and followed his suggestion, then crossed to close the shutters on the windows that faced the ocean. Hawk came behind her and gently placed his hands on her shoulders. Pulling away, she snapped, "Let's roll. We have to meet that contact at 10."

She next tried to twist away from his touch, but he wouldn't let her go.

"He won't evaporate," Hawk countered firmly but gently.

Cholly had to will her body to stiffen in his arms, when all she really wanted to do was turn around and hold onto him as if her life depended on it. She didn't know how

100

she was going to endure being cooped up in the squad car with Hawk all day. But she did know that she couldn't afford to fall in love right now. And that given half a chance, Hawk would break her heart and not even know he was doing it.

Hawk brushed his lips across her silky black hair, then released her with a tender but sad smile.

She knew she could have handled the situation if he had acted as she expected him to, but his gentleness could prove to be her undoing. Her mind wanted to panic, but then the law of self-preservation kicked in. She would just take a page out of the male survival book.

Cholly swung her purse over her shoulder and marched to the front door. With one foot already out the door, she turned and remarked, "Look, Hawkins, you're reading more into this than you should. As I said before, we were trapped in a sexy setup …."

"No one forced you to do that version of the hula …."

"Damn straight." As she turned her heart and head away from him, she wondered, "How do men pull this off?"

"I have to admit, that was poor judgment on my part. But all things considered," she stepped across to the iron gate before delivering the coup d'etat, "under the circumstances, any man would do."

# Chapter 25

When they reached the car, the radio was paging them. If was a cryptic message: another body had been found with a piece of the Missionary Collection near it.

As the partners pulled into the parking lot at Queen Emma's Summer Palace, Hawk felt a sense of almost overwhelming sadness. The lush grounds were well-manicured into a serene, park-like setting. In its midst was a charming, small white and green trimmed Victorian house. He felt it was obscene to have this tranquil beauty marred by the ugliness of a violent death.

When he shared his thoughts with Cholly, all he got was a grim-lipped, "Yeah, well there's never a perfect place for murder, is there, Sergeant?" There was a brittleness to her tone that caused Hawk to turn and look at her.

Cholly had taken on a pinched look; an almost gray pallor seemed to flit across her features. They got out of the squad car, but Hawk put a hand on her arm and stopped her from going up the path.

"What's wrong?"

Cholly drew in a breath that seemed to fill her whole being. She nibbled at her lower lip for a second, then remarked in a whisper, "Sometimes … do you ever feel … like you've just … seen one body too many?"

Hawk nodded, then put his arm around her shoulder and gave her a reassuring squeeze as they moved silently up the narrow walkway.

---

The killer waited for the newscast. A chuckle of satisfaction filled the room when the announcer recounted the newest developments. Are these serial killings or not? The latest victim was socialite Abigail Bingham.

---

Cholly had bagged the pewter dish and stood pensively slapping the package against her palm. "What the hell was going on here?" she wondered to herself.

The porringer had the same ink markings on the bottom as the other dishes did, so it must have come from the Missionary Collection.

Despite media hysteria, from the beginning the police had not seriously considered these as serial killings. While there were the similarities of the caliber of bullet and the Collection items, true serial killings almost always had sexual connotations.

The latest victim was not shot. And serial killers don't change weapons.

Hawk had been examining the body. He stood up, made some notations in his notebook, then moved over to where Cholly stood deep in thought.

"What do you think?" she asked absentmindedly.

"Rough guess: poison."

"Um ... how long do you think she's been dead?"

"You testing me, Lieutenant?"

"In our climate, rigor mortis sets in differently than it would in Boston."

"Fair enough. I'd make a guess at 12, maybe 14 hours."

"While we were at the luau?" A very uncharacteristic shiver ran through Cholly's body.

"Could be. Makes you think doesn't it."

"I think maybe I'm tired of thinking."

She moved over to the body, hunkered down and gave a professional look at the "remains." From her early days on the street, Cholly had always hated that word. Too often that was a very apt description of what was left for them to deal with. "I know I've seen this woman in the social pages, but she seems familiar-looking from something else. I wonder what it was?" she mused.

As she continued to examine the body, her subconscious began working on its own, and she suddenly sat back and looked at Hawk. "This is the lady who was in the photograph we found of Kamuela and his brother at some event. I'm sure of it."

"I really wish this had been just a simple little heart attack," she added. Gingerly she lifted the once pristine lace collar of Abigail's print dress. The tiny flowered pattern was very similar to ones found in the museums. No sign of a bullet hole was hidden in the dried vomit.

Cholly looked at the ashen face. The color was certainly compatible with certain types of poisonings.

"Lieutenant, we've gone over the place very carefully. The only thing unusual is the dish. There isn't even a cigarette butt or ticket stub in the driveway." The officer seemed disappointed, as if somehow it was his fault there wasn't anything lying around.

"Did you check the trash containers?"

"Yeah, they were emptied just before the place closed for the night. We're talking zip, nada."

Hawk came back from his own inspection of the grounds. "There isn't even a twig out of place." Again he put his hand on Cholly's shoulder. "Let's grab a bit of breakfast while we wait for the post mortem. There's nothing more we can do here."

# Chapter 26

The killer had spent a restless night and was up at dawn. The dishes and thermos had been washed out, then smashed with a hammer and discarded in a dumpster behind a supermarket. Even if they were found, there was nothing to link them with Abigail's murder.

---

The dead woman's attorney, Horatio Randolph Leighton, was off island and would return later in the day.

"Well, let's go ahead and start with the housekeeper."

Mrs. Hudson sat dabbing her eyes and heaving great sighs. She was a robust-looking woman in her late 60s with a slightly plump frame.

"I know this is hard on you, Mrs. Hudson, but it's very important that we get as much information about Miss Abigail's movements as possible." Cholly gave her a sympathetic smile. "I know you want to do everything you can to help us catch her killer."

"Oh, lordy, yes, ma'am. Such a sweet, kind soul. I'm so glad you're here. The officer who came to tell me she was ... gone, couldn't tell me anything more." Fresh tears erupted from Mrs. Hudson's eyes. "Miss Abigail wouldn't hurt a fly —"

"Yes, Mrs. Hudson, but the fact is that someone did kill *her*. And we need your help. Please tell us, did she have any problems with anyone, have any enemies?"

"Oh, Sergeant, no. We keep — kept — pretty much to ourselves. I dealt with all the tradesmen. About the only people she ever saw were old friends, that is, what was left of them."

"We understand that she made a habit of going up to spend time at Queen Emma's. That she liked to sit and read in the garden. Do you know why?"

"Of course. She said it reminded her of more genteel times. Also, Queen Emma was godmother to one of her great-uncles."

"Mrs. Hudson, how did Miss Abigail get there? We didn't find a car in the parking lot."

"Oh, Miss Abigail never drove, never even learned. When she was a child, they had a chauffeur. In later years, I drove her places before my rheumatism got my knee so bad."

"Then how did you ladies get about? Go to the store, meetings, parties?"

"Well, now, that is simple. She hired a man to drive us. Billy Wong used to take either one of us where we had to go."

"Then he drove her to the Summer Palace?"

Mrs. Hudson covered her mouth with her hand and got a stricken look, as if she'd been caught in a lie. "Oh, dear, I forgot. He had to go off island for a few days. She took a cab."

Hawk consulted his notebook. "Mrs. Hudson, we were told that she didn't arrive until about 30 minutes before closing time. She was still sitting in the garden when the guard left. Doesn't that strike you as odd?"

"How so?"

"If she arrived in a cab, how would she get a ride home if the museum was closed, if she couldn't call for a cab?"

"Why with her friend, of course."

Cholly and Hawk looked at each other, then Cholly asked, "What friend?"

"The one who asked her to tea." Mrs. Hudson looked from one to the other as if they were a little dense, then finally added, "Didn't I tell you about that?"

"No, ma'am, you didn't."

"Oh, dear, this has all been so upsetting … let's see … oh, yes. Several days ago she received a note in the mail. It wasn't signed but it said an old friend had come back to town and wanted to meet her for tea in the garden of the Summer Palace. She was as excited as a school girl. Changed her dress three times, she did …." Her voice trailed off and was replaced by a fresh batch of tears.

"Mrs. Hudson, do you have any idea as to who that friend might have been?"

She sniffled and shook her head, but then stopped and seemed to focus on something. "I remember once, years ago, when her cousin came over from Maui to visit. It was when I first came to work for Miss Abigail. This cousin brought her lady's maid with her. A real gossip that one was. When the cousins went out at night, she insisted on coming into the kitchen and spending the evening.

"Well, one night she got to talking about why Miss Abigail never married. Seems when she was in high school, she fell in love with a local boy. Her folks didn't think he was good enough for her, so they shipped her off to relatives on the mainland and she never saw him again."

"Do you know his name?"

"No, and this girl didn't know it either, just the story." Her eyes grew wide with speculation. "Do you think he's the one who killed her?"

"No, that's pretty unlikely. He had almost 40 years to harm her if that had been his intention. This cousin, does she still live on Maui?"

"Heavens, no, she died, oh it must be at least 10 years ago. None of Miss Abigail's family is still living here in the Islands."

As they left the house and walked down the path to the car, the two officers exchanged exasperated looks. "We sure can't take that information to the bank," Hawk grumbled as he eased behind the wheel of their car.

"You're right, and it doesn't make any more sense than the other murders. Here's an old lady who no one has any reason to murder, yet she's sayonara and another damn piece of the Missionary Collection is left next to the body. At this rate, maybe I'll just take early retirement."

# Chapter 27

Sitting in the den, the killer reflected on the events leading up to this murder, as well as the actual act. The killer had visited all the gourmet food and tea specialty stores searching for just the right blend of tea. Because of the highly toxic nature of oleander, there was no way to test camouflaging the taste. "Perhaps mixing several flower-scented, aromatic ones would do. And just for good measure, I could add extra flavorings. That should hide whatever taste the oleander might leave."

Wearing rubber gloves, the killer had pulverized a cupful of the deadly flowers, then added some leaves for good measure. The result was a fine powder that mixed easily with the teas from the store.

Abigail Bingham had always loved the Queen Emma Summer Palace. Normally, she spent part of one afternoon a week sitting quietly in the garden, some of the time reading, other times just enjoying the solitude. When she received a note asking her to meet an "Old friend in the back garden at five for tea," she was intrigued.

When she was a student at Punahou, she had dated a very special young man. They had only a brief time together before her parents broke it up. They told her they didn't feel he was suitable for someone of her station in life. Abigail was sent to a university on the mainland and lost track of her suitor.

Something about the note she had received made her think of him. She had spent hours going through her wardrobe trying to find a suitable dress; she had been like a school girl getting ready for her first date.

The summer house and gift shop were closed; the docents and guard had left for the day. Because Abigail had taken a cab, no one realized she was still on the grounds. Five o'clock came and went and she was still alone. As the shadows in the garden deepened, she had become apprehensive. How foolish of her to indulge in this fantasy. She had just decided to go out onto the highway and walk to the nearest house when a white car had pulled into the parking area.

Someone had gotten out and reached back to bring out a picnic hamper. As the figure moved nearer, she realized it was a person wearing a long cape and a large hat that shadowed their face. When he, or she, was within a few feet of Abigail, she had seen that the face was painted white like a mime's.

A shiver of fear had run through her, but the other person quickly smiled and gestured warmly to the bench, and lowered the picnic basket beside her. With a flourish, the mime had opened the basket and produced a heavy white damask napkin, which was gently spread out on her lap. Next, a plate of exquisite pink-flowered petit fours had been removed from the basket. The figure had held the plate of tiny cakes out toward her. Then Abigail relaxed and joined in the spirit of the adventure. She took the plate and bit into one of the sweet cakes.

With a steady hand, her mystery host had poured a cup of tea into a delicate china cup. A great fuss was made of adding honey from a tiny crystal pitcher; it was then stirred in with a delicate demitasse spoon. Abigail was handed the cup, at which point she asked coyly, "Aren't you going to join me?"

A silent nod was accompanied by pouring out a small amount of the liquid. Her companion raised the cup in salute, then slowly rested it against the white lips.

111

Giggling like a schoolgirl, Abigail drank deeply of the fragrant refreshment. Her cup was refilled, but she didn't realize that her companion's cup remained untouched.

She was urged to drink again, then the mime signed that something was in the car and moved away. The killer moved toward the parking lot to see if it was still empty. Traffic whizzed by on the Pali Highway carrying people in a hurry to get to Kailua. No one was paying attention to the closed tourist site.

Looking back through the trees, the killer could see the drama had started to unfold. Abigail clutched her stomach, letting the cup and plate of cakes fall onto the grass. The woman moaned softly, then crashed to the ground, writhing in agony. Silently, the killer returned everything to the picnic basket, ignoring the prostrate woman. Before closing the basket, a gloved hand extracted a round object and laid it next to Abigail — a child's porringer made out of antique pewter.

# Chapter 28

Horatio Randolph Leighton looked as forbidding as his name. His white hair was long, almost in sideburns. Gray eyes, the color of cold steel, greeted the detectives with as much warmth as that metal exuded. Even before he "harrumphed" at them, Cholly knew that would be his response to their presence. He gestured to the two maroon leather chairs that faced his desk, then leaned back slightly in his own.

"My secretary tells me you require some information about my deceased client, Abigail Bingham." He looked at his watch, then back at them with an air of disdain. "I have a meeting at the State Capitol. I can allow you 15 minutes, no more."

Years of experience had taught both officers to deal with every kind of emotion or reaction. If Leighton had thought he was going to intimidate them with his attitude, he was dead wrong.

Cholly nodded to Hawk to begin and she sat back to study the attorney through almost closed eyelids.

"When we spoke to the housekeeper, Mrs. Hudson, she indicated that the deceased did not have any relatives living in Hawaii," Hawk began. "Is that correct?"

"Yes. Those members of the family that are left live in several cities in New England."

"It also appears that Miss Bingham did not have many friends in Honolulu."

"Throughout the years she had been very active socially. But being elderly herself, most of her contemporaries have passed away. She dined out with friends occasionally, my mother and I at least once a month, but basically she spent the last few years living very quietly. Although now that I think of it, she did go out to certain charity functions."

"To your knowledge, did she have any enemies?"

The attorney gave Cholly an almost indignant look. "Really, Lieutenant, a woman of Miss Abigail's stature. We are not talking about riffraff here; she was a genteel -- "

Hawk interrupted him with, "Everyone is capable of having enemies, sir. Maybe a disgruntled ex-employee, perhaps even a tradesman who didn't serve her needs satisfactorily."

Cholly almost choked on his words but knew exactly what he was doing.

"No, absolutely not! Besides, she was killed by a serial killer, we all know that."

"Oh, do we?" Cholly did little to hide a slightly sarcastic tone to her words. "For your information, Mr. Leighton, we have never seriously considered these killings to be the work of a true serial killer."

The attorney snapped forward, his hands clasped tightly together on the desk. "Then who?"

"You tell us." The older man blanched at Hawk's words.

"I — what — what could I possibly know about her murder?"

"Well, for openers, tell us about her beneficiaries. Murder requires a motive, as you should know. Who stands to gain the most from her death? Nieces, nephews, Mrs. Hudson, perhaps even you?"

At that, the attorney went almost ballistic. His face turned red and Cholly wondered if the man was going to have a heart attack. "I resent that remark, Sergeant. My firm is one of the oldest in the Islands. My family also came over as missionaries. They were part of the Fourth Company, for your information. My reputation is above reproach."

"Still, your firm is in charge of her affairs. You do receive a fee for your services. If it turns out you are her executor, you may be administering a very large estate." Cholly crossed her arms and leveled an intimidating look across the desk. "Let's make this very simple for all of us. You get out a copy of her will so that we know who stands to benefit from her death. Then you can fill us in on current business transactions, if any."

Leighton took out a handkerchief and dabbed at his forehead. "Well, I don't know ...."

"Mr. Leighton, you seem to forget we are investigating a homicide. We can do this here, or you can come downtown with us."

Leighton pushed the intercom. "Miss Murakami, please bring in the Bingham file," he ordered. The secretary appeared within a minute, handing him a thick folder.

Hawk opened his notebook to a new page. The attorney shuffled through a few of the top papers, then announced, "There are no business deals, as you put it, Lieutenant. While the family's original wealth did come from real estate, upon her father's death Miss Abigail

115

instructed me to liquidate everything and invest her money in stocks, bonds, mutual funds, that type of thing. She derived her income from 'clipping coupons.'"

"May we please have the names and addresses of the heirs?" Hawk poised the pen over his notebook, but Cholly glanced at the paper in the attorney's hand.

"It looks like quite a long list; how about photocopying it?" Her smile was as false as the attorney's cooperation.

"Miss Murakami," he almost roared. When she entered, he gave her his instructions, but Cholly interrupted him to request two copies.

Hawk had to fight to keep a straight face. This was a new side to the boss lady. She might deal him a fit, but she certainly was never boring.

For the next few minutes they studied the list of obscure relatives. The housekeeper was the only other person mentioned as an heir.

"Mrs. Hudson told us she had been with Miss Bingham for almost 45 years. Was there ever any bad blood between them?"

"Oh, heavens, no. On the contrary, she was as much a companion as a housekeeper. When Miss Abigail was younger and traveled a great deal, Hudson always accompanied her."

"Let's get down to some specifics, Mr. Leighton. What happens to the house and its contents?" Cholly glanced at Hawk out of the corner of her eye. She wondered where he was going with that question.

"Well, the relatives will have the right of first refusal. If one of them wishes to occupy the house, it will revert to them, but Miss Abigail thought that was highly unlikely. They are also welcome to claim any piece of furniture or objects d'art as long as it is for personal use, not to sell."

"And the remainder?"

"Will be turned over to the Mission Houses Museum. She had hoped they might turn her home into a branch of their operation. It is a classic example of the grandeur during the last decade of the monarchy."

Hawk raised an inquisitive eyebrow. "What if they could not use it in that manner?"

"Then they are granted permission to sell it and use the funds for Museum purposes."

"What about the furnishings?"

"They would be distributed between various museums: the Mission Houses, of course, Iolani Palace, the Bishop."

Hawk frowned at the list. "But nothing for Queen Emma's Summer Palace?"

"No, except for a monetary bequest."

Cholly looked at Hawk, who then asked, "Don't you think that is a bit strange?"

"No, why should it be?"

Hawk flipped back a few pages, then commented, "According to the gardener who found the body, Miss

Bingham was a frequent visitor. Several times a month, sometimes more, she went out there and sat in the garden reading. If it was such a favorite spot, why wouldn't she donate some of her family treasures to them?"

Suddenly the attorney seemed to brighten and puff up with renewed authority. "My dear sir, if you knew anything about Island history, you wouldn't need to ask such a stupid question." His tone sounded like a history professor talking down to an inferior. "The items at Queen Emma's belonged to the royal families. No matter how exquisite some of Miss Abigail's pieces are, they would be totally inappropriate there."

Hawk was not thin-skinned, but he bristled inwardly at the man's tone. He didn't dare look at Cholly, as he was sure she was getting a kick out of his dressing down. He was wrong.

"I do not appreciate your rudeness to my colleague, Mr. Leighton." Hawk turned to face Cholly in surprise. For the first time, he saw what some of the patrolman had called her "Iron Lady" mode. "For your information, Sergeant Hawkins comes from Boston and some of *his* ancestors are the very ones who probably financed your ancestors' mission here. However, since some of my ancestors were on the shore to greet them, I win. So put a sock in your snobbery and just stick to the facts."

"Really, Lieutenant, you needn't be so nasty —"

"Mr. Leighton, murder is a nasty business. And you seem to be forgetting that someone deliberately killed your client, a woman who you claim was also a friend. And just for the record, unlike a clean, fast gunshot, being poisoned is a nasty way to die."

# Chapter 29

Hawk loved the dawn. No matter how lousy yesterday was, or today might be, most mornings he felt as if he had been reborn. Of course, he already had some doubts about maintaining that positive attitude while riding along with his partner. But for the moment, he was going to forget Chan and just enjoy being alive.

The cryptic message regarding "Yellow Bird" the other day had given him a flashback to a problem he'd been working on, but for the moment it had been dealt with and he could relax and enjoy his morning run.

Honolulu was a jogger's paradise and no matter how early Hawk started out, he always found people on the paths. It was still dark out and the breeze from the ocean had a fresh, exhilarating tang to it.

Hawk had always loved the water. When his parents were killed in a plane crash, he went to live with his grandparents at Stonecrest. Life on the estate was solitary, but the beautiful ocean-front mansion afforded the youngster a chance to make his own place in the world as his elderly relatives really didn't know what to do with a lively six-year-old boy.

The servants were kind, often spoiling him with treats, but there was still no one he could turn to, no one to establish a close relationship with, no one to confide in. So the ocean became his friend. Before he could drive a car, he had his own boat.

He spent endless hours aboard, reading, sailing and daydreaming. Some of those dreams were wistful, wondering what life with a real family might have been like. Early on, Hawk decided he wanted the whole nine yards: wife, children, the vine-covered cottage. Corny, maybe, but it would be a real home.

Every Thursday and Sunday was cook's night out and they went to the country club for dinner. He tried not to envy the children who were there with parents and siblings, but sometimes it was a battle he lost. Hawk did appreciate the fact he had a good home with people who cared for his welfare, but it just wasn't the same.

A natural athlete, Hawk was invited by the tennis pro to join the junior team. He declined, never having felt the competitive edge that most people need to excel in sports. He was big for his age and didn't need to prove himself in a physical way or use sports to be accepted. But when the club formed a fencing team, Hawk became excited about something other than sailing.

As Hawk puffed up Diamond Head Road toward the lighthouse, he smiled in remembrance of the long hours he ran along the Charles River, trying to strengthen his legs and improve his breathing. When he made the final cut for a spot on the U.S. Olympic Fencing Team, Hawk was ecstatic. But fate threw him a curveball.

He had been encouraged to apply for a prestigious Rhodes Scholarship. Hawk planned to submit his application for the year following the Olympics but there was a mix-up somewhere along the way, and he was accepted for the same year as the games.

Hawk was very frustrated, torn between two desires. Again, there was no one for him to turn to for advice.

In the end, it did not matter, as fate decided for him. He lost his concentration during a fencing match. And although the foils were not supposed to be sharp, his opponent slashed his forearm in an accident that no one thought could happen. Since the wound couldn't heal in time for the Olympics, Hawk headed for England and life at Oxford.

Hawk stopped at the lookout point near the Diamond Head Lighthouse and sat down on the lava rock wall. Dawn whisked through and the morning sun now warmed the scene. The ocean looked calm enough to skate on. A lone inter-island cargo ship sliced through the smooth surface, plowing its way toward Maui.

He drew in a deep breath, savoring the sweet smells of the clean morning air mixed with the gardenia-like aroma from the nearby tiare bushes. "This really is paradise, but it's still got garbage like the rest of the world," he mused.

Hawk leaned back on his arms and raised his face to the sun. He didn't want his mind to go there, but he couldn't help feeling a twinge of guilt for leaving his last assignment, the Organized Crime Task Force.

But Hawk had felt he didn't have a choice. He'd spent too many years chasing the Triad, the Chinese crime syndicate. As an undercover cop, he'd lived in the sewers of life, under constant pressure. Finally, major burn-out developed to the point that he was afraid he might become a menace to himself and his comrades.

And then there was Allyson. Her attitude hadn't helped the situation. Even now, he could hear her strident voice trying to cajole him into doing her bidding.

"Really, Woodrow, I don't see why you must be so stubborn. All this nobility. You can still 'serve humanity' by going into Daddy's firm. Lawyers take pro bono cases all the time; do that if it will make you feel better."

Hawk pictured the quintessential Eastern Seaboard debutante with her blonde hair clipped in the latest fashion, and uniform approved by Vogue.

They had had their last argument on the deck overlooking the club's marina. Repeatedly, Hawk had tried to make her understand him, that he was not and never would be her idea of the perfect Boston gentleman.

"Honey, I know I'm making you unhappy, and I am sorry. But you have to see where I'm coming from." With a pained look, he turned and swept his arm toward the whole club area. "These people. This lifestyle. It's so empty ... so meaningless."

"But Woodrow, you grew up here. These are your friends ...."

"No, Allyson, they're *your friends*. They bore the hell out of me."

"Well, if you feel that way about our ... my friends, then you must feel the same way about me."

"Oh, Ally, that's different." He had moved closer to put his arms around her, but she drew away.

"Don't call me Ally. As a matter of fact, just don't call me period ... until you come to your senses."

An early morning bus taking snorkelers to Hanauma Bay popped its gears as it crested Diamond Head Road. The sound brought Hawk back from his reverie. Had that scene taken place only a few weeks ago? He shook his head as if to clear out the memories. Suddenly, it seemed as if they had happened in another life. With a smile of relief, Hawk slid off the wall and started back down the hill.

122

He arrived back at the apartment feeling a runner's high, but his mental mood was still frustrated. They were just treading water with these murders. While he was more than accustomed to dealing with dead bodies, life with the Organized Crime unit was far different from routine homicide.

Quickly stripping off his jogging shorts and shirt, Hawk jumped into a cool shower. Afterwards, rummaging in his drawer, he came across the lava lava that Cholly had presented to him after the first time she saw him at work in his Boston-proper suit and tie. "Why not go native when you take off your stuffed shirt," she quipped, tossing him the short, male version of a brightly printed sarong.

Hawk tied the skimpy material around his waist, then wandered into the kitchen. His fridge was a goldmine of tropical fruit drinks. He debated between the sweet guava and the tart lilicki, or passion fruit. Selecting the latter, he moved out onto the lanai and flopped down in a lounge chair facing the crescent of Waikiki Beach. There was time to relax for a few minutes before he had to dress for the office.

Hawk leaned back, adjusted the pillow behind his neck and concentrated on enjoying the soft, swishing sound of the waves breaking on the beach below his apartment. His mind had begun drifting when the exotic tinkling of the door chimes brought him back to reality. Wondering who could be calling this early, he yanked the door open with a curt, "Yes," then found himself staring.

"Allyson! What in the name of …."

She dropped her flight bag and threw herself at him. "Darling, I was on my way to Bangkok and decided to stop by and surprise you. Of course, I'll only be here for a day,

123

but I'm sure we can make the most of it!" Before he could react, she wound her arms around his neck and pulled his head down for a long, passionate kiss.

Caught off guard, Hawk started to return her kiss, then stopped and held her away from his body. His initial puzzlement at her sudden appearance was quickly replaced by a sense of annoyance.

"Okay, Allyson, what's going on here? Last month you said you never wanted to see me again; so why are you here?"

Breezily, she pushed past Hawk and moved into the living room. "Oh, darling, don't be so difficult. And for heavens' sake, get me a drink. Something cold." She threw her linen jacket on the nearest chair and whirled around the room as if she was appraising it. "Hm, very nice. It could use some upgrading, of course, but I suppose good decorators are hard to come by sitting here on an island in the middle of nowhere."

She had followed him to the kitchen. "Well, this looks like your kind of place. With your penchant for cooking, you should be very happy here."

Hawk handed her the juice, then topped off his glass.

"Here we are, darling, just like old times," Allyson purred. Raising her glass in a salute, she added, "To us."

"I didn't know there was an 'us' any more. I seem to remember an ultimatum. And I'm still a cop."

"Oh, well, maybe that wouldn't matter so much after all. You are a sergeant. It shouldn't be too long before you get promoted, then you can sit safely behind a desk. Cheers!"

Allyson drained her glass, squeezed Hawk's arm, then moved toward the lanai. "I must say, this is a gorgeous view." She turned back and looked at him mischievously. "Of course the room I'm simply dying to see is your bedroom."

Her voice became husky and she slithered over to him in her best attempt at a sexy come-on. "I've missed you." Despite the fact she usually projected a brittle and often strait-laced debutante persona, Allyson did shed all of her inhibitions in bed.

Gently, she tugged at Hawk, but he wouldn't move.

"Allyson, whatever we had is over." Hawk tried to sound disinterested while ignoring the heat of her body pressed next to his. "I'm a street cop and that's where I intend to stay. I'm never going to fit into the mold you want me in."

"Oh, darling, let's talk about this later."

Allyson again tried to lead Hawk toward the bedroom, but there was no budging him. "I can't believe you don't want me as much as I want you." She ran a long, lacquered nail across his stomach, then inched her finger upward to seductively curl it in the soft, bronze-colored swirls of hair that covered his chest.

Hawk breathed deeply, fighting the latent chemistry between them, but he would not give in to it. There was more to life than sex, and sadly he had come to realize that sex was all he and Allyson had in common.

He moved his hand up, covered hers, then pulled her toward the lanai. He led her to a chair, then moved away to stand by the railing with his back to her, his gaze riveted on the horizon. "There's no point in starting something we can't finish."

"What do you mean by that?"

"How many times do I have to tell you it's over? Allyson, we can't go back. There isn't anything to go back to."

"But that's not true, darling. I've done a lot of thinking about us, soul-searching, if you will. And now I'm perfectly willing to let you have your silly little career if it means that much to you."

"How nice of you." Hawk's voice dripped with sarcasm. "But you're not listening or you don't seem to understand; I don't need your approval, or anyone else's."

"My, my! Aren't we the aggressive one now. Oh, I like that, darling. It really turns me on —"

"Stop it, Allyson! Stop all this damn game playing."

"What's happened to you, Woodrow? You've changed. And I don't think I like the new you."

"Actually, it really doesn't matter any more what you do or don't like. I haven't changed, I'm just telling it straight. I don't want the lifestyle we grew up in. I never liked it and won't pretend I did."

Disbelief clouded her face. "Don't tell me you want to spend the rest of your life in this — this —"

"Paradise? I might. Or I might not. Either way, it doesn't concern you any more."

Allyson studied him through half-closed eyelids. She was not accustomed to losing. And seeing him half naked in that sexy wraparound reminded her of what else she would be losing in addition to the Hawkins' wealth and social position. Her scheming mind kicked in, trying to figure out what tack to take to bring him to heel.

Suddenly a chill ran through her. Had he found someone else? What was it his grandmother said when she spoke to her just before leaving Boston? Something about Hawk's phone call, some reference to problems with a native girl?

"Surely you're not interested in someone else?" she blurted out. "Maybe like that little native girl?"

Hawk couldn't figure out what she was talking about. "What? What girl?"

"The one you work with. I spoke to your grandmother just before I left. She said she had talked to you —"

Hawk's laugh cut across her speech.

"What's so funny?" she demanded.

"Boy, did you get a wrong number, dear heart. First of all, that 'native' girl, as you call her, is the toughest lieutenant I've ever had the misfortune to work with. Next, she's not a girl. She's a woman who hates men in general and me in particular."

Not sure how to approach him now, Allyson reverted to type. "Oh, darling, this is all so-o-o-o boring. Be a love and refill my drink."

When Hawk returned, she put her drink on the table and again plastered herself against him. She had made up her mind she would not take "no" for an answer. Maybe she'd cut short her trip to Bangkok. Perhaps she wouldn't go at all.

# Chapter 30

By the time Hawk got to the station house, he was more than a little out of sorts. As if Allyson's sudden appearance wasn't enough to set him off, he'd had a lousy night. Conditioning had taught him to sleep anywhere, any time, but last night had been a toss-and-turn special. Even his pleasant run and a long, cool shower hadn't perked him up mentally.

Three cups of coffee later, he was still dragging. The last thing he needed was a bright-eyed, bushy-tailed partner in his face. Before she got within three feet of his desk, he could see Cholly was brimming over with enthusiasm. She gave him a smile that would send a diabetic into a sugar coma. He didn't know what was going on, but instinct warned him she'd probably cooked up something new to bedevil him with.

"Hi, Shorty, howzit?"

Hawk stifled a groan and took a big gulp of coffee. If she had at least waited until nine o'clock, maybe he could have dealt with this case of terminal perkiness. Hawk just grunted as she plopped down on the corner of his desk.

"So, Sarge, you get settled in the new apartment yet?" She handed him a paper napkin that had grease seeping through. "Here, try this. It'll perk you up."

"What is it?"

"How come you always want to know what stuff is, malihini? Live dangerously. Go with the flow and all that jazz."

"With you, Lieutenant, life can be very dangerous." He opened the napkin and saw a greasy doughnut without a hole. "I'm not really into sweets," he began.

"Eat."

Hawk took a bite. "So, now what? Do bells go off, or what."

"No, smart guy. But now, if someone asks you if you want a malasada, you'll know what they're talking about. It's the Portuguese national food, more or less."

Hawk didn't buy into her story completely. She definitely had the look of someone fattening up the proverbial lamb for the slaughter. Cholly went to her desk and stood shuffling papers around for a few minutes.

"By the way, Hawkins the Third, how do you feel about baseball?"

"I can take it or leave it."

"Well, how about taking it? Kam's been coaching a Little League team from one of the projects. Sometimes I go along, but I really don't know much about the technical end. The dad who was supposed to fill in for him has to work so I guess it's me or nothing. They have a big game tonight and I could sure use some expert help."

At last, he saw the reason for her nicey-nicey routine. "I told you, I'm not that hot about the game. I'm far from an expert."

"Yeah, but you're a man. You're born with that stuff. It's in your blood. It's a guy thing."

"That, Boss, sounds like a very sexist remark."

"So, sue me." Her glibness was replaced by sincerity. "Look, I need help on this. The Sharks are a nice bunch of kids, so do it for them if not for me."

"Why not ask one of the other guys, maybe someone who has a kid who's into baseball."

"I tried. Everyone's busy —" She bit off the last word in embarrassment. Hawk gave her a withering look and turned his attention to some papers on the desk.

"I'm sorry. I would have asked you first, but I figured —"

"You figured what?"

Cholly cleared her throat, then spit it out. "You were too stuck-up to hang out with those kinds of kids."

Hawk studied her intently for a moment. He was rewarded with her looking uncomfortable. Finally he asked, "What makes you think I'm that big a snob?"

"I was thinking more in the line of stuffed shirt. I can't picture you getting sweaty or dirty."

"Since when do coaches get dirty?"

"Oh, you know what I mean."

"No, Lieutenant, I don't. And maybe that's part of our problem. Half the time I don't know what you mean."

Cholly was beginning to feel like a prisoner in the interrogation room. She stuffed her hands in the back pockets of her pants and wandered around the desk. "I guess it's hard to think of you as 'one of the boys,' just plain folk."

"I can live with that. I guess I don't exactly fit into the Island mode, but I certainly am willing to help out some kids. When and where?"

Cholly blew out a sigh of relief. "Six o'clock." She handed him a slip of paper with the directions to the baseball diamond.

The morning dragged by. A trip to the medical examiner's revealed that Abigail had been poisoned as they suspected, but the material would have to be sent out for analysis. Since they needed to check out a variety of seemingly minor details, Cholly and Hawk split up.

---

It was almost 6:15 p.m. and Cholly was doing a slow burn. Hawk had made her a promise and now it looked like he was reneging on it. Since the season was half over, the boys basically knew the plays, but they still needed someone to call the shots. Gamely, she did her best to get the kids started.

The game was well underway when Hawk showed up. Cholly was steaming but he silenced her with, "There was an accident on H-1 and I couldn't get off." As he talked he eyed the score and sized up the teams.

The other team was already ahead 6 to 3. Within a few minutes it became obvious to Hawk that the opponents were bigger and had more experience.

"Do something, Hawk. These kids have the heart, but they just can't seem to connect."

Hawk took his eyes off the field to study his partner. Cholly was wearing a blue team shirt and white shorts. Her hair was tucked up inside a baseball cap. She looked about 16 and as woebegone as the kids.

"I warned you —" the crack of the bat signaled that Jay, a member of the Sharks, had made contact with the ball. Cholly and the boys cheered him on, but their joy turned to dismay as the boy tried desperately to outrun the third baseman. "Slide, slide," Hawk's voice boomed over the others. Jay heard him and practically flew under the other kid's legs.

It was hard to tell who was more excited, Cholly or the team. To Hawk's surprise, she gave him a hug after Jay's run.

"I thought you didn't know anything about baseball, Number Three."

"That isn't what I said. I merely remarked that I could take it or leave it."

"I think I'm gonna owe you one, Number Three."

# Chapter 31

The next morning, Cholly finished early interrogations and came up empty. She had been fighting great uneasiness in regard to the way she had handled the situation with Hawk. She felt she had done the right thing, yet fought a sense of guilt. Felling that she owed him something, she remembered they had been discussing decorations for his apartment.

When he had asked her to suggest the names of places he could go, she hadn't intended to buy him a present, but now she decided that he descrved a gift.

Visiting one of the shops she had recommended to him, she narrowed her choice down to a wall hanging of dried leaves, flowers and fabrics for his den wall, but wasn't sure if that might be a bit too esoteric for his tastes.

When she expressed her reservations to the clerk, the clerk asked a few questions about the gift's recipient and his taste. Cholly hadn't expressed more than a dozen words when the girl interrupted.

"Lieutenant, your friend wouldn't happen to be a big, gorgeous blonde from the mainland, would he?"

The remark caught her off guard, but she nodded and asked, "How did you know —"

The girl gave her a flushed look and laughed. "We've been drooling over that dreamboat ever since he walked in the door. He bought several pieces, then debated between that hanging and a large basket from the same artist. He's been in several times. He loves that type of thing."

Cholly paused in front of the door to Hawk's apartment. Suddenly she wondered whether she should have called first instead of just arriving unannounced. "Since I'm just dropping it off, it can't matter too much," she rationalized as she pressed the buzzer.

A tall, winsome blonde in a blue caftan answered the door. Automatically, Cholly double-checked the number on the door as the woman gave her a cool, "Yes?"

"I — is Sergeant Hawkins in?"

"Yes." The woman sized up Cholly and the package, then added, "Come in." She turned her head and called over her shoulder, "Darling, there's a delivery person here to see you," as she continued to stare at Cholly.

"What did you say —" Hawk had come out of the bedroom, the lava lava draped precariously low on his lean hips. His face seemed flushed and his look was what his partner usually referred to as "slept in."

He did a double-take when he saw Cholly, then turned to appraise the blonde's reaction. She was like a statue, her eyes narrowed, and he thought her long crimson nails looked like they were ready to turn into claws.

"Why, Lieutenant, this is a surprise. Come on in. Oh, this is my friend Allyson Wentworth. She was traveling to Bangkok and just dropped in on her way. Allyson, Kaloke Chan."

Allyson's jaw dropped and her tone was incredulous. "This," she gestured to Cholly as if she didn't exist, "this is your boss? You've got to be kidding!" She turned back and studied Cholly as if she was studying a specimen under a microscope.

There was a charge of tension between the two women that was almost visible. Cholly realized that this must be the woman Hawk had been engaged to, but from the look of them, past tense seemed like a misnomer.

Cholly remembered her mission and handed the package to Hawk. "I found something for your wall. The girl at the gallery said you'd already admired it ... I think the colors ... will do ... will work in there ...." She turned toward the door. "Sorry to have bothered you."

"Hold it, Chan. Come on in and let's see how it looks." Hawk reached out and pulled her sleeve.

"I don't want to interrupt ...." She had caught Allyson's glacial look.

"You're not interrupting anything. And I appreciate your taking the time to find something for me. That was very nice of you." He was being so formal, Cholly thought she'd scream.

Wordlessly, Allyson followed them into the den. When Hawk unwrapped the mostly brown-colored hanging, she didn't hesitate to express her opinion. "My God, what's that? It's dead looking."

Cholly wanted to deck her — obviously the woman was a card-carrying bitch — but if that's what Hawk wanted, there wasn't anything she could do about it.

"Actually, my dear," the words had a bite to them, "I almost bought this piece myself. The trouble with you mainland types is you only see things in color, or one dimension. Out here, everything has a soul, some kind of beauty." His smile took the sting out of his tone. "You just have to know how to look for it. Isn't that right, Boss?"

Cholly could only nod, as she was speechless, a rare condition for her. Hawk was quoting her verbatim, yet she would have sworn he hadn't paid the least bit of attention to any of her remarks, Island-wise.

"Yep, that looks really ono, mahalo nui loa, ma'am." It was hard to tell who was the most surprised when he leaned down and kissed her on the cheek."

"My, my, my, aren't we just the cozy ones." Allyson sniffed in disdain and flounced off toward the living room.

"I'm sorry, Hawkins, I didn't realize you weren't alone —" She could see into the bedroom behind him and the way the bed looked. "Otherwise I would never have dropped in —"

She was embarrassed and bolted out o the apartment as quickly as she could.

---

The killer walked over to the Hawaii State Library, which adjoins the grounds of Iolani Palace. "What better way to spend one's lunch break than doing scholarly research," thought the killer with a chuckle. "I just need to find out more about serial killers to make sure there have been no errors."

# Chapter 32

"You're late! Where have you been?" the Captain practically growled at Cholly.

"I had to check out a new angle, but it proved to be a dud. I called in and told Manu what I was doing, so why are you so hu'hu?"

"It's that partner of yours."

"What's he done now?"

"I don't know, but I know I don't like it."

"Well, that sure makes a lot of sense."

"For openers, where the hell is he? You guys think this is a country club?" He glanced down at her jogging suit and running shoes. "Boy, when you decided to get out of uniform, you went all the way, didn't you, Chan?"

She brushed off his remark and answered his question about Hawk. "He had an unexpected guest come in town, but I know he was going to check some more of the gourmet shops for the tea —"

"I'm not talking about that," he said as he handed her a note. "Here." He shoved the pink telephone message slip under her nose. It was addressed to Hawk and told him to meet someone named Pauly in a warehouse at Kakaako.

"Do you know who this Pauly is?"

"Nope, unless he's someone left over from the organized crime case. Maybe he's his snitch."

"I don't think he's had time to make that kind of contact. It smells like three-day-old fish to me."

Cholly felt a stab of fear clutch her middle. Part of that area was a bad section of town. Some buildings were being torn down and rebuilt for urban renewal projects. But this address was along the docks and most of those buildings were deserted, at least for honest purposes.

She stood up, checked her gun and extra clips, then added unnecessarily, "I'll check it out."

"Be careful, it could be pilikia."

"Trouble seems to be Hawkins' middle name."

---

Cholly cruised the perimeter of the area in her car. There were very few businesses still operating in this part of town. The street she was looking for was deserted; the only sounds were the wind whipping at loose boards or sections of the corrugated roofs.

Although the city administration had been trying to relocate many of the homeless to the tent housing in Aala Park, Cholly knew some of the men still hung out in these deserted buildings.

Hawkin's car was parked near a rundown warehouse that had once been a furniture manufacturing plant. Debris littered the ground around the entrance. As she eased in through the narrow opening, Cholly realized the place was a minefield of broken boards, boxes, pipes and shattered glass.

She paused, straining to hear voices, but the only sound was the wind rustling through the broken windows.

139

She inched forward, cautiously looking at the floor, then upward. The rubber soles of her running shoes touched the neck of a bottle and she pulled back before it rolled out from under her foot and she lost her balance.

More than one Nam vet lived in these surroundings and they had the art of booby-trapping down to a science. Her eyes swept chest high and upwards. A few feet ahead of her was a rope that looked like it had been just carelessly tossed aside. She gave it a wide berth.

Some boxes were piled high across the aisle. The way they were arranged encouraged someone to simply push through them. Carefully, Cholly slid one sideways. Through the opening between the boxes, she saw a thin piece of wire stretched taut between two pillars. "Yes, sir, Number Three, you certainly picked some nice little boys to play with," she thought grimly.

It took Cholly a few more minutes to reach her destination, an office that was situated in the middle of the main floor. Open at the top, it was surrounded by four partitions, wood on the bottom and glass on the top. She could see a short man in a seaman's coat. He had his back to her, but there was no sign of Hawk.

The man was talking to someone, his tone angry. Cholly eased over to a steel pillar. Recessed steel rungs formed steps and she carefully climbed upward.

When she had moved high enough to see into the room, she stifled a gasp of dismay. Hawk was lying on the floor, a bloody wound on the back of his head. She heard the thud before she moved and saw the man had kicked Hawk in the side.

Cursing a blue streak, he kicked the unconscious policeman again. Whoever this guy was, he was obviously out to kill Hawk. Fear for him paralyzed Cholly and her mind went blank. Normally she reacted automatically, not needing to think of what she should do. But now incompetence washed over her.

She bit her lip until it bled, then gave herself a mental shake and got back to work. Cholly studied her possibilities. From this position, she could not help Hawk; she had to move closer. But the man had a clear view in all directions, and the floor was too littered with papers and other debris for her to sneak up on him.

Her eyes swung upward. Steel beams crisscrossed the area. Two of them were within inches of the man's head. All she had to do was walk across one of them, stop and get the drop on him. It was the perfect solution … yeah, right, walking across a beam 12" wide.

Her mind raced. There had to be a better solution. Again she heard a thud and this time Hawk moaned. She didn't have time for another solution. Cholly took out her gun, sucked in several deep breaths, and inched forward.

"I shouldn't have knocked you out right away, you bastard. You're gonna pay for busting my brother, but I'd like this better if you could feel the pain —"

"You can't even imagine the pain you'll feel if you don't take two steps backwards — *now* you son of a bitch."

The man was confused. He whirled around looking for the voice. Cholly was close enough to see the deranged look of fury on his face. He could flip out either way. "Now!" and she fired a warning shot two inches away from his foot. So much for protocol.

He backed up, but still held onto his gun. "Unless you want to talk like a soprano, drop your gun and kick it away." He looked upward, then arched the gun toward her. She shot it out of his hand. "I let you off easy, but just give me an excuse —"

Hawk had awakened. Despite the pain, he saw his tormentor standing with his back to him. Calling on his last bit of strength, he kicked out, catching the man across the back of the knees and pitching him forward. He tried to flop onto the man's back to get handcuffs on him, but he couldn't make his body move close enough.

He heard a light thump and saw a flash of bright blue nylon in front of his eyes.

Cholly put a knee on the man's neck, jerked his arms around and snapped the cuffs onto his wrists. "Allow me, Number Three. I think you've had it for today."

Hawk tried to focus his eyes on her and just before he lost consciousness, he quipped, "You're back in blue, I see."

# Chapter 33

The Captain arrived with the paramedics. They tried to convince Hawk to go to the hospital. "Look, this isn't the first time I've had my ribs broken. They don't even tape them up any more, so why bother?"

"Did it ever occur to you, Mister Macho, that you might have a concussion?" Cholly's tone was laced with anger, but Hawk ignored it. He grabbed her hand and said, "Hold up some fingers." She realized he wanted to see if he could focus his eyes.

The paramedic moved her aside with a "Let me."

The Captain and Cholly stood by while he gave Hawk a cursory examination. "He probably has a mild concussion; we'll take him —"

Hawk persisted, "I'll be okay. I've had those before, too."

The Captain shook his head, then growled, "You go — and that's an order. And Cholly, you go along to be sure he doesn't bug out on them. I'll come by when we finish up here."

---

The X-rays and examination were over and the emergency room doctor was cleaning Hawk's head wound when the Captain arrived. "Wow, what did he hit me with?" Hawk winced.

"I found a bloody two by four near you; it was even splintered — you've got a hard head," Cholly answered.

As if on cue, the doctor handed Hawk a sliver of wood. "Here's a souvenir if you want it. You're darn lucky." The antiseptic brought out an "ouch," then the doctor applied a bandage.

"Okay Sergeant, that should do it. We'll just keep you overnight for observation —"

"No way, doc. Just gimme my shirt and let me out of here."

Cholly and the Captain exchanged puzzled looks at the vehement tone. The doctor turned to them. "Captain, talk some sense into your man. A concussion needs to be monitored; he has to be checked out for at least the next eight hours."

"Fine, I'll go home with my partner and she can do whatever's necessary. How 'bout it — will you watch over me, Mommy?" His grin would have been lascivious, except he obviously was in pain.

"Let Allyson watch over you."

"She's gone — for good."

At her look of disbelief, he said, "Really, I mean it. We're pau."

She smiled at his choice of words. Cholly wondered why she felt like a weight had been lifted off her heart. It must be the aftermath of the warehouse fiasco.

He cajoled, "Well, Mommy, please, I don't want to stay in the hospital —"

"I'm not running a convalescent home —"

"You took Kam in."

"That's different."

"Yes, I know." The words were so quiet, Cholly could barely hear them.

Cholly looked at the Captain for moral support, but all she got back was a cheery, "Hey, that's the way it should be. You know the rules. You save someone's life, you own it."

---

Hawk leaned on Cholly as they walked the few steps to her front door. Once inside, she moved him toward the guest bathroom, then started taking off his bloodied shirt.

"Boy, Lieutenant, your timing stinks. If you wanted to ravish my body, why did you wait until I'm all busted up?"

Cholly just pulled a face at him and concentrated on keeping her hands from shaking. To take her mind off his physical presence, she asked the questions the doctor had instructed her to. "Where are we?"

"In heaven."

"Don't be a smart ass."

"Alone with you in your nice isolated house is as close to heaven as I expect to get."

"Well, at least you know where we are. What month is this?"

"January." He winced as her fingers accidentally grazed his bruised side. She bit her lip, feeling his pain as if it were her own.

When Hawk reached down to unzip his pants, Cholly felt weak in the knees and she quickly turned away to walk over to the shower. "Are you going to scrub my back, too, Mommy?" he asked innocently.

"I'm going to wash your mouth out with soap if you don't behave, Woodrow. Now, who am I?"

"The Dragon Lady." She turned and gave him a frosty stare. "My mommy? No. Okay, how about my boss, the very perfect Lieutenant Charlotte Kaloke P.S. Cholly Chan. Anyone who can run off that mouthful has no problem with their memory or a concussion."

She started to make a remark, but he hooked his thumbs inside the waistband of his shorts and she beat a hasty retreat, accompanied by his triumphant laugh.

While Hawk was in the shower, Cholly tried to pull herself together. She puttered around the kitchen, dropping silverware, pulling out the coffee, then spilling it when she tried to fill the basket. A mental tongue-lashing was in order.

"You told him to get lost after your little romp on the beach, so what's with this weak-kneed bit? You can't have it both ways, girl. You know he turns you on, and it's obvious the feeling is mutual, so why not go for it?" Cholly slammed the refrigerator door on her finger and cussed in every language she knew.

"Oh, shut up. You know why I won't let myself go." The little voice got sarcastic. "I know why you think you shouldn't let yourself get involved with him, but that's a crock."

"No, it isn't. You know he's hung up on all that vine-covered cottage stuff and I wouldn't be caught dead buying into that kind of deal … at least not for a few more years."

"By the time you get around to it, sweetie, you'll be looking for husbands in the geriatric ward."

This internal argument was interrupted by, "Hey, Mommy, where are my clothes?"

"I put them in the washer. Use the robe on the back of the door."

She was putting juice and rolls on the lanai table when he joined her. While the peach-colored terrycloth robe wrapped all the way around his body, lengthwise it left a lot to be desired. The hem was above his knees, and long, muscular legs moved with a sensual casualness.

Cholly took a deep breath and moved back into the kitchen. When she returned with the coffee pot, she had all she could do to keep her hands from shaking. Hawk reached up and took it from her, then asked, "Why are you limping?"

"I landed wrong." At his quizzical look she added, "I jumped down from the rafters."

His look of disbelief was followed by a loud laugh, but then he broke off and looked deeply into her eyes. "Thank you, Mommy." His touch was as soft as his tone and she didn't realize he intended to kiss her until his lips covered hers.

Oh, it felt so good to be in his arms again. She knew she shouldn't do this, but just for a second — what harm was there in just a few moments of pleasure? "Plenty," said the little voice in her head, urging her to pull away.

"Please, Hawk, we shouldn't —"

"Why not? You just saved my life —"

"Don't be melodramatic —"

"Okay, I saved yours —"

"Like hell you did; I would have —"

"Oh, shut up — " and he made sure she did.

---

It was almost sunset and Hawk was still asleep. Cholly was curled up on the bed next to him. She had spent the most bittersweet hours of her life watching him sleep off his ordeal. Periodically, she lifted his eyelids, flashed a small penlight in them, saw them react as the doctor had ordered, then let him sleep on in peace.

With a feather-light touch, she traced one of the ominous bruises on his side. Oh, God, if she hadn't found him …. The thought of Hawk's being killed made her start to shake again and she moved to snuggle up along his side. Instinctively, his arm reached out and curled around her, and for the first time all day, she relaxed.

"Hi, Beautiful." He brushed a kiss across her neck, under her ear. "I had the most wonderful dream, but I was just wondering, was it a dream?" His head had ended up on her shoulder, his hand resting lightly on her breast.

Cholly longed to spend the rest of her life in exactly this spot, but again the little voice inside nagged at her.

"It's just your adrenalin acting up. You know, a reaction to your injuries," she replied.

"Oh, so how come you're in bed with me, then?"

"You were restless, crying out in your sleep … and I had to keep checking your reflexes; it was just easier to stay with you —"

"Liar!" His kiss was as sweet as a vintage wine and Cholly just wanted to give in and admit her love for him, but her mind and her heart were on a collision course.

As he eased his body over hers, she whispered, "No, we can't; please Hawk, we shouldn't —"

"Why not?"

"You're hurt."

"Not that badly."

"But I don't want to be hurt."

He moved his head back to look at her closely. A mist of tears covered her dark eyes and he felt as if he could see into her soul. "Oh, Sweetheart, don't you know I'd die before I'd ever do anything to hurt you? Trust me, Love, it will be all right."

# Chapter 34

The killer was depressed. Abigail's death had cemented the serial killer theory, at least in the mind of the public, but his research had shown that true serial murders usually involved more than three victims. Did he need to pick a fourth victim plus another way to kill the person? This was getting to be so much work!

A feeling of restlessness overcame the killer and the shadowy figure started pacing the darkened room. Trying to sort out his feelings seemed to add to the sense of agitation. Finally he stopped pacing and poured himself a drink from a crystal decanter sitting on a small tray table by his chair.

He crossed to a bookcase and took down a richly-embossed leather-bound photograph album. Moving back to his chair, he sank down into it and opened the book. He fingered through it, not really stopping to look for anything in particular, just examining whatever page he paused at.

He lingered over an old photo that depicted two young boys astride ponies, the younger one smiling as if he didn't have a care in the world. The older boy was slightly behind him, a solemn look on his face.

"Always in the background. Photos, affection, it never changed." A deep sigh filled the room. The only sound was pages being turned, until he stopped and peered closely at a formal picture. "Ah, dear Papa. Well, I hope you're satisfied. Your precious baby son has joined you — I wonder if it's in heaven or hell?"

Suddenly, he jumped up, the album falling to the floor. He ignored it and started to pace again, then abruptly left the room.

The staircase curved upward, with a large landing halfway up. The walls were covered with formal paintings of family members. The killer stopped on the landing and gazed up at the dominating picture of his grandfather. For a few moments, he stood quietly, like a schoolboy waiting for a lecture. His face took on a troubled look, then a defiant one.

"Well, Grandfather, I hope you appreciate what I've done for you. That miserable wretch was ruining everything you built. He didn't care about the land, the companies, only debauchery — but you needn't worry any more — he won't cause any more trouble — your empire is safe now."

His voice trailed off and he suddenly broke out in a sweat. Of course, there was *his* debt. But he'd take care of that. Now he had no one to answer to. "Yes, Grandfather, I've made sure everything will turn out all right."

# Chapter 35

Keo MacGregor pulled his taxi into line under a tree near the end of the parking lot at the Ala Moana Shopping Center. He smiled, remembering how much money he made yesterday. The rain had started early in the morning and continued all that day. Ala Moana was mobbed. True, most of the fares were short ones — tourists loaded down with packages and not wanting to fight the bus crowds to go back to heir hotels in Waikiki. But he'd still had a good day's take.

The weather this afternoon promised to be picture-postcard perfect and the beaches would be crowded. He hoped his day wouldn't be just short rides to Waikiki, that he could get some longer fares.

---

Cholly bounced into the office, then stopped several feet away from her desk. With a practiced spin to her wrist, she sailed a piece of ivory-colored cardboard into an arc that landed in Hawk's lap.

"Here's a job that just has your name written all over it, Number Three."

With his thumb and forefinger, Hawk lifted a heavily engraved invitation into view. He assumed a pompous tone of voice as he read the information out loud. "The pleasure of your company is requested at the Black and White Ball." He raised a questioning eyebrow, "I heard you talking about it, but just what *is* the Black and White Ball, Boss Lady?"

Cholly slid into her chair and gave him her best Cheshire cat grin. "It's Honolulu's primo social event of the year, Sarge. All the hoi polloi will be there. You should feel right at home. Of course, it is formal. You can always rent ...."

Hawks sarcasm matched her own. "I'll borrow my grandfather's ... but why am I ...?"

"We."

"Are we, going?"

"Well, for openers, my father's not in the mood, so he's palmed it off on me." A flicker of surprise crossed Hawk's face, but before he could hide it, she snapped, "Yes, believe it or not, Number Three, my family is socially acceptable. But more importantly, Cap thought it might be a good chance for us to snoop around — unofficially, of course."

"Does he still think someone at the Palace is involved in these murders?"

Cholly slapped the file that rested in front of her. "There has to be some connection, no matter how loose it is. People can't just walk in off the street and grab a piece of the Missionary Collection. But I'm damned if I can figure out how they're doing it."

"Do you honestly think we are going to find an angle during a charity ball?"

"Probably not, but it's a free meal. And they usually have a good orchestra. You *do* dance, of course. Miss Hooty Tooty's dance school, no doubt."

"Actually, we called it a Cotillion, ma'am. And I can get around the dance floor without stepping on a *lady's* toes. Course whether that will apply to you or not, only time will tell."

Cholly made a face at him, but didn't give her usual sarcastic remark, as she was beginning to get used to his teasing.

"I just hope you're not the kind of date that needs a week to get ready. After all, the ball is tonight," she added.

Hawk raised an eyebrow and remarked, "Do you always give your dates so much notice?"

"Hey, gimme a break, Number Three. My father just decided he didn't want to go. So I got elected to represent the family. But, if it's too much trouble for you, I'll just go by myself. In the meantime, we've got an appointment with the registrar at the Palace."

Before the detectives could leave for the Palace, their boss came out of his office. He walked into the squad room and slammed a newspaper down on Cholly's desk. "Maybe you guys should start a scrapbook. 'Course, it's going to be pretty redundant. 'No comment' or 'we're looking into it.' Those the only two expressions you know?"

Cholly didn't know what had set him off, but she really didn't need this grief right now. She was aggravated enough for both of them. For the first time in her career, she looked, and more importantly felt, like a fool. She didn't have a perfect record, but she always got up to bat. This time she mused that she couldn't even seem to *find* the ballpark.

Hawk was trying to placate the Captain when, without comment, Cholly got up and motioned him to follow her.

"Where you going?" Cap bellowed.

"To the Palace."

"Why don't you get a cot and just stay there?" came the sarcastic suggestion over his shoulder as he moved back into his office.

"Maybe we will, *Uncle*." Much to Hawk's amazement, Cholly stuck her tongue out at the Captain's back, then marched to the door.

# Chapter 36

Driving a taxi was one of Keo's two jobs. The other was working for the North Shore stables. He loved animals and wished the stable job could be a fulltime one, as he had always had a special touch with horses. Suddenly his face lost its smile, and an air of gloom threatened to ruin his day. What was going to happen to him now?

The six horses of Mr. Winslow were the backbone of the stable. Polo ponies needed a lot more specialized care than rental nags. Old man Morales could probably handle those himself. Damn, why did Winslow have to go and get himself killed?

An old man, obviously a tourist, settled down on a bench at the big glass-enclosed bus stop next to the shopping center. There was a large crowd waiting for the numerous buses that stopped there. He eyed the throngs, then glanced over at the taxi stand, a thoughtful expression crossing his face.

Keo looked at his watch. It was just a few minutes after three o'clock. One last fare, maybe a trip out to Pearl City or Hawaii Kai and his shift would be over. Of course, those long hauls hardly ever happened, but it didn't cost anything to dream, did it?

Out of the corner of his eye, he saw the old man approaching the line of taxis. Definitely a tourist, this one, with his cheap, gaudy blue and yellow aloha shirt hanging out over faded tan chinos. He clutched a Long Drugstore sack and ABC plastic shopping bag in his left hand. Both were stuffed to the top, probably souvenirs and gifts for the folks back home. He gripped a cheap wooden cane in his right hand.

There was one taxi ahead of Keo's and he hoped the guy took it before he moved up to his turn in line. Probably a short ride to one of the cheaper hotels in Waikiki.

The cab ahead of Keo pulled out to the signal of a man standing near one of the stores, and the old man shuffled toward him. He wore a wide-brimmed, pale blue cotton hat that had "Hawaii — Oahu — Molokai — Maui" stenciled on it in bright blue and red letters. The brim was pulled down low and sunglasses hid most of his face, which was starting to show a stubble of whiskers. The man had long white hair that had a funny sheen to it, but Keo didn't pay too much attention, as he was ticked off at the thought of having to go on what would probably be a short trip with little or no tip.

"Where to, mister?"

"Well, I don't know."

"I can't drive you if ...."

"No, you don't understand. I want to look around the island. At first, I thought I'd take one of them bus tours, but they was going to places that was too touristy for my taste."

"Well, what do you want to see?"

"The other part of the island — away from the city, maybe. Of course, I do want to go to Pearl Harbor and the Cemetery of the Pacific; I got buddies in both places."

"Okay, but I'm going to have to check with my dispatcher first. That kind of tour could take three, maybe four hours easy if we go to the other side of the island. And it could be expensive."

157

"Don't worry about that — I've got the money." He pulled out a worn leather wallet and fanned through $20 and $50 bills.

"Okay, Pops, just let me check in."

# Chapter 37

The registrar greeted Cholly and Hawk with a pleasant smile. But when they told her they wanted a list of everyone who had ever donated any items of value, it turned dour. "Oh, you've got to be kidding. Under the best of circumstances, what you're asking for would take up a great deal of my time. And with the ball tonight, we are all very busy; there's no way I can help you —"

"Excuse me, Mrs. Lee, but you don't seem to understand. The information we need is not something optional. It's part of an ongoing murder investigation. You don't have a choice. We need it. And as soon as possible." Hawk softened his command with an engaging smile.

The woman frowned, then remarked, "Even if you are the police, I have to obtain permission —"

Cholly waved her toward the door. "Anything you need, but let's get on with it."

"If it's really such a hassle, should we check it out ourselves?"

"Oh, Number Three, you are a glutton for punishment. They don't have those records in the computer. Do you have any idea how tedious it will be trying to cross-check who donated those pieces and all the possible tie-ins?"

"I sure do, but I also know we have a better chance of spotting a pattern or connection than she does."

"Agreed, but we can do that from the lists she makes, capish?"

"My Italian is rusty, but I guess I agree."

Within a few minutes, Mrs. Lee had returned, breathless and slightly agitated. "I guess I have no choice but to do as you request, but if you're in a hurry then you'd better plan on helping me."

The rest of the day was spent in excruciatingly boring research. They split up the inventory lists dating back to the time period of the pieces from the Missionary Collection. Since the items from that Collection were not segregated as to a certain timeframe, they had to read literally all the information on each object on the list.

When they had finished, they thanked the registrar and left with a pitifully small list for the time involved.

"We may have a date for tonight, but it looks like we have our work cut out for us."

"I can't believe these lists. It'll be like unraveling a Chinese puzzle."

"Maybe not." Cholly looked at the few sheets of paper in her hand, then stuffed them in her pocket. "But it will go faster if we go somewhere quiet and lay them out on a table. The office is too distracting."

"Your place or mine, Lieutenant Honey?" Hawk gave her a lascivious grin.

# Chapter 38

"This sure has been an interesting trip; you make a good guide, Keo. Maybe you should do that for a living."

"Yeah, well I may have to change jobs soon, so I'll think about it. Where to now, Pops?"

The old man pulled a rumpled-looking list out of his shirt pocket and studied it for a second. "My grandson said to go to the Pali Lookout. He says it's 'awesome.'"

"It sure is a great view, man, but it's kinda late now."

"But it's not dark yet."

"No, but I don't know how much you're gonna be able to see when we get there."

"Okay, you warned me, but I won't get back to Hawaii again, so let's try it anyway."

As usual for early evening, the parking lot was deserted when they pulled in off Nu'unau Pali Drive. The wind in the 1,200-foot-high gap was fairly strong and the old man had to hold onto his hat as they walked the short distance to the precipice.

Keo felt nervous. Normally, he wasn't a superstitious person, but this was the site of a bitter victory in the battle for Oahu. History was not clear as to whether the troops of the defeated King of O'ahu jumped, or were forced over the edge by Kamehameha the Great, but either way, they fell to their deaths on the rocks far below.

Keo had just enough Hawaiian in him to believe that spirits lingered in such a place. And the Kua'p'io — the Night Marchers, a group of spirits — were said to march in the valley.

"Don't take too long. It can get dark up here real fast."

"Where do those steps lead to?"

"Another sidewalk that runs along on a lower level."

"Let's go see the view from there. Will you help me down the steps? My leg's getting tired."

Keo was uncomfortable, but put his arm under the old man's and led the way to the lower level, ending up next to the waist-high retaining wall.

The man nodded in satisfaction. "This should do quite nicely. His tone of voice made Keo look up in time to see a gloved hand reach out a metal cup to him. "I thought you might like this."

Keo took the cup and studied it for a minute. "What for?"

"As a souvenir."

"Of what?"

An eerie laugh echoed through the oncoming dusk. "Why, of your horse career — all those phony veterinarian bills, duplicate supplies, yes, all those years you bled my stupid brother — but now it's your turn to bleed."

Before Keo could react to this statement, the flash of a knife blade lunged forward, stabbing him in the stomach again and again.

# Chapter 39

The invitations to the Black and White Ball advised guests to park in a lot several blocks away from the Palace. They would then be driven to the party in horse-drawn carriages. The entire event was based on parties the last king, David Kalakaua, had given.

Because she was actually going to a beauty shop, Cholly told Hawk to meet her at the parking lot. Although he had arrived a few minutes earlier than the agreed-upon time, he realized that they would be among the last guests to be transported to the ball.

As he paced under the shade of a jacaranda tree, he wondered what kind of date Cholly would make. Her uncanny ability to change with almost any setting was impressive, but it was one thing to blend in with hoods and criminals, quite another with the Café Society set.

"Lord, Hawk, you sound like your grandmother now. Don't tell me after all that ranting and raving about Allyson's 'crowd' that you really are a snob at heart," the little inside voice said. A purple blossom fell off the tree, and as he brushed it away, he shook his head as if to clear out any such thoughts.

Looking at the flower made him remember Cholly's refusal of a corsage. Her, "You're in Hawaii, brah," didn't satisfy him, but he was too tired to argue. He pulled back the heavily starched white cuff of his dress shirt and looked at his watch. Talk about being fashionably late.

Several cars had pulled in at the other side of the lot. He noticed an older couple coming toward him, followed by a vision in white chiffon that literally took his breath away. The woman was tall and slim as a reed. Her black hair was swept up in elaborate swirls. Woven in-between the curves appeared to be a strand of pearls.

As she moved closer, Hawk's blood pressure jumped several points. The dress was fashioned with an intricate halter top. The soft, clinging material was pleated upwards from the waist. The chiffon had been draped in a way that cupped each breast into a sensuous mound.

While the skirt fell into soft folds, it gave the effect of clinging as she almost slithered toward him. Unconsciously, he ran a finger around his suddenly too-tight collar. In an effort to take his mind off her walk, he studied the garlands hanging from her hand. One looked like a green vine and the other a white necklace, but as she moved closer, he realized it was an almost lace-like lei.

The couple smiled a hello and moved into a waiting carriage. Hawk had offered the woman an arm up, and when he turned back, he had the shock of his life.

The vision in white was only inches away, and it was Cholly. Her perfume seemed to seep out of her exquisite hair and envelop him in its warm embrace. Before he could blink, she slipped the green vine around his neck, and kissed him on the cheek, as was the custom when bestowing a lei.

"Aloha, Number Three. You look like the groom on the top of the wedding cake." She eyed him appreciatively. "You didn't say Grandpa owned white tie and tails."

Hawk was too stupefied to say anything brilliant, so he blurted out, "They're mine. I own a tuxedo, too."

"Of course." She handed him the fragile, woven lei. Silently he took it from her, his warm fingers brushing hers. He had to reach up to slip it over her head. The fragrance

165

from the flowers was almost overpowering, and he knew he would never forget it.

"You lost two Brownie points," Cholly said a bit breathlessly.

"Huh?"

"A kiss goes with a lei, remember?"

Their eyes had not lost contact since she had put the maile leaf lei around his neck. Hawk was so mesmerized by the transformation in her that he stood statue-like for a few moments before he finally bent his head and kissed her, not on the cheek, but lightly on the lips.

Realizing what he had done, he covered his action by stammering, "You're taller."

Cholly lifted the hem of her slinky skirt to reveal very high-heeled white satin sandals. "Bridges the gap nicely, don't you think?"

The carriage pulled up in front of them. Hawk took her arm to help her up into it and gulped. The dress had no back. The draped bodice continued around under her arms and ended at the waistband. Except for the closure at the neckline, it was bare.

An unexpected explosion of sensuous heat coursed through his body and he groaned inwardly, "Oh, boy, Sergeant, this could be one long night."

It took only a few minutes for the carriage to arrive at the wide King Street entrance to the Palace. The deep green gates, topped by golden spikes, gleamed in the light of hundreds of kukui nut torches that stood guard along the driveway and up the steps to the veranda.

A liveried footman helped Cholly out of the carriage and Hawk followed her up the wide staircase, doing his best to avoid looking at that damn provocative dress. For a second, he wondered if she had deliberately picked out something that sizzling or if her indifference to the opposite sex ran over into her choice of clothes. Knowing her as he now did, she could have arrived in sack cloth and ashes if the mood suited her. And, he grumbled to himself, she'd probably look wonderful in it.

They went through a small receiving line and entered the Palace. The main hall had been smothered in flowers. Maile leaf vines, like the one Hawk wore, were entwined around the banisters that cascaded down from the open second floor hall. The walls were lined with paintings of the monarchs. The top of each picture was crowned with a swag of maile leaf vines that had been entwined with the brilliant orange of the tiny iliama leaves. Tall urns stood guard at the foot of the staircase. Armloads of roses overflowed the sides and perfumed the soft night air.

"Let's find a table on the upstairs lanai, if that's all right with you?" The smile Cholly turned on him would have melted the snow on the top of Mauna Kea. Was being dressed like a lady having some effect on her, or had she finally called her own kind of truce?

Hawk gave a mock bow and answered, "Your wish is my command, Cinderella." He followed her up the grand staircase but couldn't resist adding, "Although I think if she had arrived at the ball in that dress, the Prince would have had to stand in line to get to her."

"How gallant — and are you planning on becoming Prince Charming tonight?" Her voice had taken on a breathy quality she had never used before, but it seemed to have come out of its own volition.

167

They had reached the top of the staircase and Cholly turned to go outside. As Hawk walked beside her, he leaned down and whispered, "Maybe you'll give me a chance to show you just how charming I can be." His hand slipped under her elbow and she could feel its heat through the paper-thin white leather of her formal gloves.

Tables were placed randomly along the lanai. The majority were occupied, but Hawk spotted two seats at the end table close to the tower room. "Do you mind sitting back there? If you do, I can look downstairs —"

"No, that would be fine." They made their way to the table, introduced themselves to their fellow dinner partners and settled down to a wonderful meal. The dinner was a duplicate of one served during King Kaluakua's reign.

The pale green faille cloths were topped with assorted white-and-peach-colored roses, camellias, gladioli, tuber roses and lilies. Part of the pre-ball publicity announced that each table's flower arrangement would be displayed in an antique container from the Palace. The one on their table was a long, low oval with wreaths of flowers and garlands etched on the side. Gently, Cholly traced the pattern with a coral-shaded fingernail.

"Do you suppose Mr. X, or perhaps Ms. X is doing some shopping here tonight?" Hawk's tone was conversational, but she sensed the tension behind the question.

"I'd pray for it if he or she made a mistake and we could bust 'em." Because they did not want to be overheard, their heads were almost touching, and Cholly couldn't help but inhale Hawk's aftershave. It was new and positively the most sensual aroma she had ever encountered. There was a hint of citrus with something else she couldn't identify. She frowned as if trying to place it.

"What's the matter?"

"Nothing. I was trying to figure out what you are wearing."

It was his turn to be puzzled. "On the mainland we call it white tie and tails —"

"Not that, you dope. I mean that fragrance. I know there's something like citrus, but the other —"

"The Male Mystique."

"Yeah, right. Okay, don't tell me."

"I just did."

"Come on, Number Three —"

"No kidding. It is some fruity thing, but has a different aroma on each person as it mixes with their body chemistry. Would you like a closer sample?" he asked as he edged his chair a little nearer to hers.

"No, thank you. I'm already having enough trouble breathing right," she admitted.

"Well, I'll be damned. I've spent all this time trying to woo you, ma'am, with my overwhelming charm and all I needed was a few dollars worth of eau de cologne."

The smile Cholly gave him suddenly faded and she stiffened in her chair. Hawk noticed the change immediately. "What's the matter."

169

"I don't know. But I feel —" she ran her hand across the back of her neck as a small shiver passed through her. "Don't you feel something? — it's like — someone is watching —." She swiveled around suddenly and stared into the room at their backs. It was well lit, with people milling around, but no one was looking in their direction. She barely glanced at the darkened tower room as it would be empty. Cholly was wrong.

"Come on, let's try out the dance floor. The orchestra does sound wonderful." Gently, he drew her up and slipped his arm around her waist. He could feel a slight tremor still running through her body. While he had not experienced the same sensation Cholly had, by now he knew her well enough to believe that her instincts were almost always right.

They paused at the doorway to the room that faced the lanai. "Do you want to check it out?"

"It couldn't hurt." Casually, they moved into the room, then sauntered down to the far end and peered into the dark tower room. The shutters, which normally pushed into concealed slots on either side of the window when not in use, were pulled tight across the glass. Cholly shrugged her shoulders, then added, "I think this case is definitely getting to me."

---

The killer barely had time to slip back among the other guests. A satisfied smile settled across what became just another face in the crowd.

---

"I haven't been dancing in a very long time. I hope I don't step on your toes." Cholly felt like a tongue-tied teenager going out on her first date. What was the matter with her tonight? Since she was driving, she'd had only one small glass of champagne before dinner. She pretended she couldn't find any excuse for her state of mind, but she was just playing mind games.

She was in love with Hawk. She didn't want to be; she didn't want anything or anyone upsetting her ordered life, but as she had said to him earlier, "You can't put the genie back in the bottle." And she couldn't take back the fact that she had slept with him.

Hawk held her lightly in his arms, even reverting to using a linen handkerchief in the hand that rested against her bare back.

"Where did you come up with that one, Number Three?"

"At the Cotillion, of course. A gentleman never places his hand on a lady's bare back. But then, of course, ladies don't wear dresses like this one."

Cholly stumbled at the half-jesting insult and out of habit, she was about to let him have it, when he gave her the most ingratiating smile in the world. "Honey, don't even think of getting hu'hu. Every man in this place is dying to trade places with me."

He pulled her a bit closer. "And if you try to tell me you didn't buy it just to make that kind of an impression on me, I'll make you take a polygraph test."

Instead of flying off the handle, which he half expected, she simply stated, "We always attend the ball. I bought it long before I met you."

"You're a lousy liar." He bent and lightly kissed the tip of her nose. "You look good enough to eat, Officer Honey."

They danced every number until the band took a break. Not a word passed between them. It wasn't necessary. The spell that bound them was like a sensuous silken thread. Hand in hand, they almost floated up the grand staircase.

The dessert had been set out and they properly appreciate the white spun sugar swans filled with Strawberries Chantilly. Hawk poured out the remaining champagne, which barely filled one glass. He took a sip, then pressed the glass to her lips. Her hand covered his and for a brief second they were the only two people in the world.

Hawk felt bewildered and bemused. Just a few months ago, he truly believed Allyson was the right woman for him. And now he was caught in the spell of the most contrary, bossy, infuriating, beautiful, sexy woman he had ever known.

"You know, Cinderella," he lightly stroked the side of her face with his knuckles, "the party doesn't have to end when the ball is over. We could —"

She suddenly stiffened and her eyes widened; for a moment he thought she was going to hit him. Instead, she grabbed one of the hurricane lamps from the table and rushed to the tower window, shining the light inside as best she could. The shutters were now open. She pressed her face close to the glass, but couldn't see the figure that had hastily leaned back against the side wall.

They both knew the magical spell was broken. Still holding hands, they quietly descended the stairs and waited their turn for a carriage. The ball was over for Cinderella and Prince Charming.

# Chapter 40

When the phone on Cholly's nightstand rang, she groaned, turned over, and hid her head under the pillows. Her tired brain shrieked, "Give me a break, whoever you are." She knew, of course, that it wouldn't stop ringing. And that it would be trouble. No one she knew ever called her early in the morning for just a pleasant social chat. As she groped for the phone, she mused, "Please don't let it be more pilikia."

"Yes," she snapped, her head pounding from another sleepless night.

"Sorry to wake you, Lieutenant, this is Manu in dispatch. We have a call from Central Division; they've got a body up at the Pali Lookout. From what Montes said, it looks like it has your name on it."

Not again! "Isn't this guy ever going to give it a rest?"

She tried to brush her hair out of her eyes, but it had a mind of its own. "Manu, why does Montes think he's mine?"

"Does the word Missionary Collection mean anything to you, Chan?" The dispatcher couldn't resist a chuckle before ringing off.

Cholly picked up Hawk, who didn't look in much better shape than she felt. Wordlessly, he slipped into his seat, handed her a foam cup full of coffee, and snapped on his seatbelt. Cholly took a sip, then complained, "It's black!"

"As is my mood, lady."

She nodded and they took off toward H-1. The drive to the Pali Lookout took only 11 minutes.

She remarked caustically, "We made good time, but I'll lay you odds the photographer isn't even here yet."

The detectives pushed their way through the small crowd that had come up for an early morning view and got more than they bargained for. The wind had died down and the sun was promising another warm day. They moved down the steps from the main viewing area to the one on the lower level. As they turned the corner, Cholly let out a sigh of resignation and stopped.

Hawk was a few steps ahead of her. He slowed and turned when he realized she wasn't beside him. He came back and stood in front of her. "Cholly?"

For a second it seemed as if she hadn't heard him, but then she remarked, "No matter how many years I've been around accidents and death, the coppery smell of blood always gets to me — it is definitely not Chanel # 5." She looked up and gave him a rather pathetic smile and started to move on, but he detained her with a hand on her arm.

"What's really the problem, Honey?"

"Don't call me that."

"Yes, ma'am, but what's going on?"

She hesitated, as if trying to form the right words. "I … I … don't know. I'm just so damn fed up, so frustrated. I've never been this tired in my whole life. I get up exhausted …. I don't know what's going on anymore."

Hawk swung his head around to be sure they were still alone.

"Look, Lieutenant Honey," he said with a slightly lopsided smile, "you don't need to be Freud to figure it out. These murders could try the patience of a saint, and neither of us can pass that test. And you've got the added burden of fighting your personal life —"

"What is that supposed to mean?"

"Aw, don't play coy, Iron Lady, it's not your style. You hate to admit it, even to yourself, but you are in love with me and it's tearing you apart. And I'm damned if I know why, since you know how I feel about you. But regardless, you're on an emotional treadmill; don't you think it's time you got off?"

"Well, if you'd solve the case, Hot Shot, at least I could get one foot off." She tried to lighten up as they approached the officer standing by the body.

"Morning, Lieutenant, Sergeant." The officer looked a little gray, his mouth drawn. "We've secured the area; the medical examiner's on his way and so is the photographer." Hawk nodded approval, then turned his attention to the crime scene.

The body lay at the foot of the retaining wall on the lower level. There was blood smeared on the top of the wall, as if it had fallen there, then slipped down. The victim was lying on his side, facing the wall, so they could get only a partial view of his face.

Hawk hunkered down and leaned over as close to the body as he could, to try to see over the shoulder. "His shirt looks like someone used it for a pin cushion. With all this blood it's hard to tell, but my guess is multiple wounds all close together. He poked his latex-gloved finger at the cuff of the long shirt sleeves. "Bet we find scrapes on the inside of at least one of the forearms."

"If you think he slumped on the wall, then slid down, why aren't there blood stains on the wall?"

"If the killer was facing him, and he staggered sideways against the wall, then fell quickly —," he said as he stood up. He grinned and then pointed downward, "He's got a big opu, maybe that pushed him away."

Cholly smiled at his use of the Hawaiian word for stomach; at least he was trying. Hawk turned to the officer. "Did you check on the other side of the wall yet?"

"No, sir, we had to concentrate on this area, and keeping the people away. But I did notice when I came down on the other side that there's dried vomit on the stairs. Figured the killer lost his cookies there."

Hawk peered over the retaining wall and Cholly gestured as she remarked, "Be my guest; you're the athlete."

He walked over to a spot where there was a small amount of level ground on the other side of the wall. Lithely, he vaulted over, then carefully made his way back as close as he could to the spot where Cholly stood.

"Well?"

"Nothing. No blood, no weapon. If anything was dropped, it probably would have slipped on down into the underbrush past that smooth spot. We'll need guys with spikes to search that area."

Cholly was getting impatient. They couldn't move anything until the photographer arrived. "Where the hell is Spud?"

"Well, you know he lives up past Schofield Barracks …."

"So? It's early, and there isn't that much traffic. Get on the horn and find out what's happening." Her tone was getting frosty.

Hearing footsteps, Cholly turned to find the Captain approaching, holding a bag from a fast food chain. "Figured you didn't have time for breakfast." He glanced over her shoulder at the body. "I hope this isn't what I think it is."

"If it is, our man has changed his M.O. We've got a messy stabbing."

The Captain moved to examine the body just as the photographer arrived full of breathless apologies for the delay. "Just get it done, boy, so we can get to work," Cholly snapped.

"Okay, Lieutenant, wiki wiki." He gave Hawk a "What's her problem?" look and started snapping away.

The medical examiner arrived with his usual cheerful banter. "Yoshi, I can't deal with your terminal perkiness this morning. Go wait in the car, or here, drink my coffee. Either way, just *go*!"

The Captain came back to ask, "What's got you hu'hu, Cholly? You're chewing everyone but me; figure you're going to try that next?"

"Oh, Cap, it's this damn case. When are we going to get a break? … Or is he going to quit? Just look at that mess." She turned and gestured toward the area. "Nothing makes sense. For instance, did our victim come in that cab? All the other cars in the parking lot are accounted for." She stopped, put her hands on her hips, and looking at the murder site remarked, "What a lousy way to die."

"Never knew a good one."

"Oh, you know what I mean."

"No, I don't. As a matter of fact, I don't understand a lot of your attitude lately. And we're going to talk about it later. I'm leaving, but I'll send Yoshi back. The kid's done."

---

The killer had thought of everything, planned the moves down to the last detail. A rusty old blue truck had been hidden under banana leaves at an abandoned banana plantation, next to a construction site on the other side of the Pali tunnel. It was a simple matter to walk down to the Pali, turn right onto the highway toward Kilauha and head through the tunnel.

It took less than a minute to remove the camouflage from the truck. He covered his tourist shirt with a dusty work shirt and put on a dirty cap. If anyone had seen the truck leaving, they would have assumed he was just one of the construction workers.

---

"What would you say was the time of death?"

"Probably somewhere between seven and 10 last night. Boy, somebody sure wanted him dead. Looks like we've got at least eight, maybe 10 points of entry. I won't know for sure until I get him cleaned up. Are you finished with him?"

"No, the photographer was late. We still have to check him out." Hawk shrugged as he leaned down to start his task.

"I'll go get a cup of coffee; be back in about 20 minutes, okay? You should be done by then."

"Yeah, and if not, you'll wait," Cholly answered.

She pulled her gloves on and started on her side of the body. Hawk had pulled the man's wallet out and had started through the contents. Cholly looked under and around the body, but couldn't find any signs of a piece from the Missionary Collection. The dispatcher couldn't have been wrong.

"Hey, Jensen, come here." The other officer, who had been on the upper level with the crowd, hurried around to the steps and came down to them. "The dispatcher told me when you guys called this in, you said there was another piece from the Missionary Collection. Where is it?"

"Sorry, Lieutenant, with all these sightseers up there, I got distracted." He moved back to a curve in the wall where they had placed a blanket, rolls of yellow tape and other assorted tools of their trade. He lifted a corner of the blanket and came back with a plastic bag which he held out. "It sure is a funny-looking cup, not like the other ones."

Hawk took it, turned the bag sideways, then handed it to Cholly. "It's a stirrup cup."

180

"A what?"

"Stirrup cup. They're used by the horse set, usually at fox hunts. They bring drinks out to the riders just before they start." He stopped, then went on in a phony English accent, "A bit of scotch to take the chill off the bones this morning, m'lord?"

"Don't tell me you rode to the hounds, Number Three?"

"Well, ma'am, I did go to school in England —"

"How jolly for you."

"Actually, I went out only twice. It wasn't my thing. But getting back to business, something doesn't track here."

"Like what?"

"You don't have fox hunting in Hawaii."

"Of course not."

"There is some hunting on the Big Island, Sergeant," Jensen added.

"But that's not the kind he's talking about. Of course in the old days, the Alii did hunt, and sometimes they had guests. There were a lot of English here at one time."

"That's it. These are from England. It's an old tradition. Or you might find them in the south; they used to be big on fox hunting, but not in —"

They said, "New England," together.

"Of course, Number Three, you're right. The Missionaries wouldn't have had something like this. Even if they had ancestors who had been into the fox hunt scene, the only things they brought with them were more everyday necessities."

Hawk turned the cup over again. "And there are no ink identification marks on the bottom."

"Could they have washed off, sir? There was a shower up in this area around midnight."

"Maybe, but some museums use special ink that doesn't come off easily with water."

"Well, ma'am," Hawk bowed slightly from the waist, "are we a happy camper now? We finally found a clue, of sorts."

She held out her hand for the cup, then nodded, but added with a sigh, "I suppose this means we'll have to go back to the registrar at the Palace."

"Frankly, I doubt it. We didn't find anything on the other list, and this is definitely not Missionary material."

"More importantly, this is a big break. Even if it is an offbeat serial killer, they don't change weapons. This has to be a copycat murder."

Silently they worked on, each absorbed in the search for clues. In the man's wallet, Hawk had found a plastic card holder with a driver's license and several credit cards. A puzzled look crossed his face and he renewed his search of the pockets.

Cholly caught his look "What's bothering you?"

"If he drove that cab in the parking lot, he should have a special hack license or something. There's no ID here for that."

Cholly ignored Hawk and went back to work. Suddenly, he stood up, looked at a card, then asked her, "How many people are there in Honolulu?"

"With or without tourists?"

"Without."

"Oh, close to 400,000. But whose counting?"

"With that number, what do you think the odds are that two of the victims would know each other?"

"Small."

Hawk handed her a card, a broad smile creasing his face. "If I'm not mistaken, that's the same stable Winslow keeps his horses."

"You think this Keo is his Keo?"

"Looks that way. If he is, we have some kind of tie-in, don't you think?"

"Keo's a very popular name here, but it looks like you could be right."

"Now are you happy, Lieutenant?"

Cholly gave him a small smile. "I'm working on it."

# Chapter 41

The post mortem was scheduled for late afternoon. Cholly and Hawk got a late breakfast, made a few stops, then went back to the station. They were surprised to see the Captain standing by their desks.

"Tomorrow, the guano is going to hit the fan. Not only will the mayor be all over us, but probably everyone this side of Guam. Kids, I know you've been busting your okoles on this one, but we have to come up with some answers before I get nailed tomorrow. Let's go in the squad room and lay it out, see what you've got that I can use."

Hawk used the chalkboard to draw a tree-like outline. Using their notes as a guideline, they laid out all the information. Settling down at the conference table, the three of them studied the board intently.

"Okay, first let's look at the similarities. Only thing all four have in common is a piece of the Missionary Collection, right?"

"No, Cap, this last piece was not from the Missionary Collection."

"Okay, but three of them were killed in historical places."

Hawk interrupted, "But isn't the Pali Lookout one, too? I remember the story of Kamehamea the Great and all those O'ahu warriors going over —"

"Yeah, but that's different da kine. We know that none of them knew each other —"

"No, Cap, it looks like we have a break there. This last victim, MacGregor, worked at the same stable where Winslow kept his horses."

"Now that's more like it! Is there anything else?"

Hawk flipped open his notebook. "The manager at the cab company where this guy worked says he was a bachelor with no family; the only other place he ever went was to the stable. We went to his apartment house but the manager wasn't there, and no one was home at the other units. We'll go back later."

"Okay. Let's finish the rest. The shoe salesman doesn't seem to have anything in common with victims two and three, but those two have some fits. Both belonged to the art museums, the symphony, and they were members of the same country club. Although the Winslow and Bingham families have ties through the missionary families, neither his brother nor her housekeeper claims to know the other family, except by name." He paused and looked at his two detectives. "What else do we have?"

Hawk stepped up to the blackboard and added a notation. "Okay, we have four murders. Two were committed with a gun. Then the killer switched to poison and finished with a knife. Talk about variety."

"This is pupule! We've got a psycho offing people, but then changing MOs, and somehow getting cups from the museum. Yet we can't find any apparent motives," Cholly complained.

"Wait, what did you just say?" asked Hawk, suddenly alert.

"This is driving me nuts?"

"No, changing MOs. Maybe now we have an honest-to-God copycat killer," Hawk said.

"I suppose that's possible. We sure don't have a motive for the Brigham woman. Hell, we don't even have a motive for the first two murders," she replied.

Hawk moved over to the evidence board. "But now we do have kind of a slight connection," he said, pointing to post mortem photos of Abigail and Kamuela. "They were both in that horse picture."

"So the shoe salesman is the odd man out?" Cholly asked.

Hawk walked back to his desk, shuffled through some papers and handed one to Cholly. "Here's something else," he said. "Look at this. Young and Winslow were the same height, weighed within a couple of pounds of each other and they both had dark hair touched with gray."

"So maybe Young was killed by mistake? Winslow was the real target?" she mused.

Hawk nodded. "According to the report, it was dark during the rally. The only light was from those kukui torches. It sure would be easy to do."

Cholly sat up. "That works for me," she said. "But all we really have is that two of the victims are in the same photo."

The Captain eased over to the door. "What's your next move?"

"We're going back to the stable and dig some more," Cholly remarked as she stood up.

"Good. Keep me posted. And if you find out something spectacular, let me know right away. I'll need all the ammunition I can get for tomorrow's meeting."

"There's something that's been bugging me," Hawk began. "Hiram Winslow's name keeps showing up. I think we need to check up on him a little more. I hate them, but I think we need to do a stake-out."

# Chapter 42

The most boring police work there is often produces vital evidence. But both detectives knew they were in for many dull hours.

"I hope Winslow is still in there," Hawk commented.

"My source knows his business," she replied.

As they got comfortable in the squad car, they began talking and learning a little more about each other.

"How did you get into the Triad-stalking business?" she asked him.

"Jian Wa was my roommate at Oxford. His family had been in the export business for generations. The Triad tried to take over the company. They even killed his father. A few years after we graduated, he called me. There was an international task force being formed and he asked me to join it."

"I'll bet that thrilled your family."

"They didn't know. And my fiancé hated everything about my job, so I sure didn't tell her."

"Some relationship."

"It wasn't, and as you say here, it's pau."

Cholly attempted to explain her family. "Tutu, my Chinese great-grandmother, doesn't take guff from anyone, including Grandfather Chan."

"And you're a chip off the old block, right?"

"I don't think I meant to be that way. But I always seemed to be at odds with everyone. It was like — I don't know —"

"You marched to a different drummer?"

"I guess that's as good an analogy as any."

"Did you go into law enforcement just to spite your family?"

"That's what they thought. And I can't be certain that there isn't a little truth in that; all I really knew was I didn't want to be a banker. I didn't know what I wanted to do with my life."

"What about that fiancé you mentioned that your family picked out for you?"

"I told my family they could kiss that cr—, nonsense, goodbye. When, and if, I decided to get married, it would be to a man I chose."

"I'll bet that went over like a lead balloon."

"Worse. Grandfather Chan didn't speak to me for years."

"And now?"

"He's mellowing. I hear he even brags, secretly of course, about what I've accomplished."

"What made you finally settle on being a cop?"

"Partly Kam, partly Cap. He's always been one of my favorite people. He loved me just for me, warts and all. My parents sent me to the mainland for my first year of college, but I couldn't stand being away from the Islands. We finally compromised. If I would spend my summers in Hong Kong and just "think" about banking, then I could go to the University of Hawaii."

"But how did that get you to police work?"

"At the beginning of my sophomore year, I took a course in criminology, just for the hell of it. I quickly found that the material fascinated me. Later, Cap and various department heads from HPD came in as guest lecturers. I was on the fence, but when Kam joined the force, that seemed to help me make up my mind."

"How did your family take the news?"

"To put it mildly, the guano hit the fan. "No Chan has ever been a policemen, etc., etc.""

"How about Cap?"

"He doesn't count, he's not on the Chan side."

"You couldn't have been more than 19, maybe 20. How did you convince them to let you go to the academy?"

She gave him an impish half grin. "You have to ask?"

He threw up his hands in mock horror. "The Iron Lady strikes again!"

"Something like that. Only I did offer a compromise. I said that after I graduated, I would go on and get my degree through night classes. Little did I know what I was undertaking."

"Did you ever have time to eat or sleep?"

"Very little, which was what lost me my so-called boyfriend."

Now Hawk feigned surprise, though he really was. "You mean Miss Man Hater had a real live gen-you-wine boyfriend?"

"He was a boy, but I'm not sure he ever qualified as a friend. And he detested my being a cop."

Hawk chuckled. "Maybe we can get him together with Allyson."

"They do deserve each other, but I heard he has a wife and three kids."

Hawk turned Cholly around to face him. "Did you become the Whiz Kid just to show them what you could do?"

She nodded and grimaced "I smarted off that I would be a better cop than they were bankers. That I would be the youngest Sergeant, and then Lieutenant, the force ever had."

"And being you, you had to prove it." Hawk shook his head, then tried to pull her into his arms. "Oh, Lieutenant Honey, I hope they broke the mold when they made you."

"Give it a rest, Number Three. Here comes Winslow!"

Hiram Winslow got into his car and drove off. They tailed him to Chinatown. He went into a Mah Jongg parlor and they set up another stakeout. They were quickly bored again.

"Are these high-stakes games?" Hawk wondered.

"Does several thousand dollars a pop sound like a game between friends?" she asked snarkily.

"If they're in the right tax bracket, it might not be a big deal.... But if Winslow usually loses, we could have our motive. He might need his brother's share of the money."

"We should go talk to Jimmy Lee. Chinatown is his beat. If he doesn't know what's going on, he can find out."

---

A few hours later, Cholly and Hawk met up with Jimmy Lee, an Asian man wearing an aloha shirt.

"Howzit, Lieutenant?" he greeted.

"Coast 'em. So what gives, Jimmy?"

"Two games in one day! He loses big, but also wins a lot. It doesn't sound like he's in over his head."

"If anything changes, or you hear anything more, let me know. You have my phone number," she replied.

"Yes, ma'am."

# Chapter 43

Hawk stopped Cholly as she was getting ready to leave for an appearance in court.

"I understand the symphony has a wonderful guest artist this week. Would you like to go to the Sunday afternoon performance? And maybe we can have dinner afterwards?"

Since the stakeout, they had been dancing on quicksand. The attraction was there. Neither of them could deny that, but it appeared that they didn't know what to do with the situation.

"It sounds good, Hawk. I really wish I could go with you. But I have to be with my family. The Chinese New Year is coming up. Once a year, I break down and cook. My sisters-in-law and I are going to make gau, under the hawk-like supervision of my mother. They we'll have dinner."

"Gau? What is that? Another national dish?"

"Sort of. I'll bring you a slice. I'm sure I would have a better time at the concert, but you know how it is." She shrugged.

Hawk was perched on the edge of her desk. As she stood up to move around him, he reached out and fingered a strand of hair that had worked itself loose from the knot on the top of her head. His voice was so soft she could barely hear him over the sounds of the office chatter going on in the background.

"From what you've told me, I wouldn't think you'd mind missing that event." He tucked the tendril behind her ear and smiled into her eyes.

Cholly couldn't take a deep enough breath to answer him. He was wearing the same aftershave as he had worn at the ball. Her policeman's mind decided it should be banned as a dangerous substance.

Hawk brushed a finger lightly along the line of her chin. "Whatdya say, kiddo? Break loose — live it up!"

The family dinner wasn't what she needed to avoid. But it was easier to let him think that than explain her fear of being alone with him. It was becoming difficult enough during the day to keep her mind on their work. She needed time away from him to recharge her batteries, defense-wise. But even as her mind acknowledged that, she felt the heat of his body drawing her toward him like a supercharged magnet.

He leaned forward and whispered in her ear, "What do you suppose our fellow officers would think if they saw me kiss my lieutenant in the squad room?" The mischievous twinkling in his eye was almost her undoing.

"Probably the same thing as when your superior gives you the knee, Sarge." Keeping her tone of voice joking was almost as hard as keeping her hands off of him. Hawk's deep laugh drew looks from the people around them, and Cholly took a half step backwards.

When she returned from court, and for the rest of the day, Hawk made remarks that she realized were thinly veiled attempts to push her into inviting him to dinner. Cholly was puzzled, as she certainly had not painted a glowing picture of the old homestead. She shook her head; if she knew that man for the rest of her life, she would

194

probably never understand him. Cholly felt the sting of tears well up behind her eyes. And why should that affect her so much?

---

The killer could not allow himself the luxury of remorse. What was done, was done. He looked at the weapon. "Yes, I guess a little ride along the shoreline would be appropriate about now."

---

Sunday dawned with a gray drizzle. Cholly puttered around the house all morning, her mood getting darker as if to match the weather. By ten o'clock, she had done the laundry and washed her hair.

The rain stopped and she took a cup of coffee out onto the lanai. Casually, she strolled up and down its length, trying to concentrate on one of her favorite pastimes, watching the ships. But instead of feeling soothed, she became almost unbearably restless.

As if her body had declared war on her head, or maybe her heart, Cholly found herself holding the receiver and dialing Hawk's number. Before the connection was made, she slammed the instrument down, then proceeded to swear in every language she knew. This man was definitely bad for her mental health.

Cholly slipped into a jogging suit and headed up her street toward Diamond Head Road. Maybe she could run him out of her system.

Two hours later, all she had for her trouble was a blister on her heel. "Oh, the hell with it," she capitulated as she again reached for the phone.

Hawk's deep voice caressed her over the phone line. "Sorry to miss your call. Please leave your name, number and message and I'll get back to you. Please wait for the tone. Mahalo."

"Give me a ring when you get back, Number Three."

Cholly stalled as long as she could. This was ridiculous. Part of her didn't want the phone to ring, the other part did. But it soon became a moot point. It was time to leave for what she had dubbed "The Fortress."

As she wound her way up to the mountaintop, the rain began in earnest. By the time she drove through the Moon Gate, which was the entrance to the paved courtyard in front of the main door, it was coming down in sheets. Cholly settled back and leaned her head against the leather rest. Knowing rain this hard seldom lasted very long, she decided to wait it out.

The garden surrounding the courtyard was a blaze of color. Crimson, white, pink and orange bougainvillea encrusted the curved walls that defined the area. Tall white-ginger plants languished under the perfumed frangipani trees. Yellow-, peach- and apricot-colored hibiscus dotted the scene.

Cholly loved all the gardens on the estate. As a child, she had spent hours reading in the different hidden area of the grounds. Some were perfumed with a variety of blooming flowers, others had been sculpted into a large green oasis.

The only cloud on the idyllic scene had been the "walks" with Grandfather Chan. Whenever she was summoned to take a stroll with him, she knew a lecture was forthcoming.

Cholly cut short her trip down memory lane. With a sigh that bordered on the aggressive, she mentally remarked, "That was then, and this is now. And I think the game is over."

Cholly had exaggerated the amount of cooking that went into making gau. After blending together the flour, sugar and oil, the mixture was wrapped in oiled Ti leaves and steamed over boiling water for several hours. The cook's main job was being sure that the water didn't boil out. How well the congealed dish set was the true mark of a good gau cook.

She enjoyed the company of her second brother's wife, Helen, who was more in tune with Cholly's views of life than Pearl, Cholly's other sister-in-law. Pearl and Cholly's oldest brother, Arnold, had moved to Shanghai immediately after their marriage. It had always seemed to Cholly that the situation encouraged Pearl to travel back in time. If the job of Dowager Empress ever came up again, Pearl was ready, willing and able to fill it.

Once Cholly finally entered the house, the atmosphere in the spacious, modernized kitchen was one of camaraderie, despite Mrs. Chan's almost fierce appraisal of water levels.

"I hear you have a new partner, Rose, a malihini." Pearl always referred to Cholly by one of her middle names.

With a half smile, Cholly shook her head in wonder. Was hers the only family that knew everyone else's business? The police department was about as far away from Pearl's domain as Mars, yet she always seemed to know every detail of Cholly's life.

"I hear he's quite a hunk," Helen added for good measure.

Mrs. Chan frowned over the top of her half glasses. "Helen, you know we do not use slang in this house." When she turned to the stove, the younger woman pulled a face at her back.

Cholly loved Helen's normal ability to take this nonsense with a grain of salt, but now both her sisters-in-law stared at her, waiting for a report.

"He's okay, I guess, but he's not Kam."

"Kam, Kam, that's all we ever hear from you. Why don't you find a real boyfriend, even a husband?" Pearl's tone was almost waspish.

Suddenly, Cholly became tired of the "broken record" speech she heard every time the family was together. She slid off the stool and moved over to the stove to check on her pan of gau. As she went to lift the lid, her mother lightly slapped her hand with a scowling, "No, not yet."

"Well, Rose, we're waiting."

"For what?"

"To hear about your new partner." Helen was brimming over with curiosity.

"No, no, you foolish girl, I mean *my* question. When is she going to settle down and act like a lady."

"Okay, that's it." Cholly turned and stared angrily at Pearl, with a little bit saved for her mother. "What does it take for you throwbacks to the Ming Dynasty to get it through your heads that *my* life does not need to revolve around a man. I do not need a man, I do not want a man --"

"So you will spend all of this life with a gun and a badge?" Her mother's tone was quiet but harsh.

"If I choose to, that is my privilege, a point which seems to be ignored by everyone in this family."

A steady stream of Mandarin filled the room as she walked out on the conversation.

# Chapter 44

Hawk tried to return Cholly's message but she was out. Glancing at his watch, he realized she had probably already left for her parents' home. He strolled out onto the lanai, trying to figure out if the abrupt message meant anything. Had she changed her mind about the concert?

Or, by some miracle, had she decided to invite him to go with her? He knew if it was connected to the case she would have been more specific.

He watched the waves for a soothing few minutes, then smiled and walked back into the living room. For some reason, it seemed Cholly didn't want him to meet her family. Maybe it was time he found out why. The common-sense part of him cautioned that she'd probably be mad as hell. His lighter side answered with: "So, what else is new?"

---

The atmosphere in the kitchen had settled down when Cholly returned to check on her gau. Her mother started to say something, but one look at her daughter's face would have been enough to warn away the gods.

In an effort to restore peace, Helen asked, "How was the Black and White Ball?"

"Very nice." Cholly knew better adjectives to describe that wonderful evening, but using them would have involved an explanation she didn't want to share.

"Oh, is that all you can tell us? I heard the decorations were awesome — I mean elegant."

"How can you enjoy going to a ball without an escort?" Pearl was on the prowl again.

"Who said I went alone?"

"Oh, my daughter actually had a date?" Her mother showed a slight sign of interest. "Anyone we know?"

"No, Mother, you don't know him."

"So, you are going to make us beg for his name, Rose?"

Many times during the years Pearl had been in the family, Cholly had fought the battle to keep from reaming her out. It was more than possible she might lose that struggle today.

"About the only thing I am going to make you do, Pearl, is mind your own business."

Undaunted, the older woman barged on. "Then you must be ashamed of him. But I am not surprised. Most men want to go out with a lady —"

"That's it. Pearl, when are going to come down off your high horse and stop acting like a bitch? I have forgotten more about being a lady than you'll ever know, sister. Just because you married into a rich family does not mean you are the social arbiter of the world."

Cholly stopped for a breath, then pounded on. "And I am sick and tired of this "lady" routine I get from all of you. Next time you think you hear a burglar, try remembering how glad you are that there are "ladies" like me around to protect you. When it comes time to add up the score, I assure you my life will have as much meaning as any of yours."

201

---

As Hawk's car wound up the long driveway, he began getting cold feet. Maybe this wasn't such a good idea after all. His plan had been to play dumb, and say he thought she wanted him to join her. Even to his ears, it rang as stupid, but he had come to accept the fact that when it came to Cholly Chan, he didn't have a brain in his head.

Hawk drove into the courtyard and parked next to Cholly's car. He got out, but then stood by the car, still debating about the soundness of his move. Before he could make his decision, the front door banged open and the Dragon Lady stormed out, followed by an assortment of men and women.

When she saw Hawk, Cholly stopped for a surprised second, then barked, "What the hell are you doing here, Hawkins?"

"You called... I thought... you changed your mind."

"Not in this lifetime, buster!" Cholly's fury at her family got sidetracked and her misplaced anger hit Hawk full force.

As she yanked open the door of her car, she raised her voice so as to include everyone in her speech. "You were all so damn curious about my new partner; well, here he is in the flesh. Meet the honorable Alexander Woodrow Hawkins III" She turned and gave them a last, furious look. "And just for the record, I think he has more money than we do." And she peeled out of the parking area.

Hawk stared after Cholly as if she had lost her mind. He thought he had become accustomed to anything she would say or do, but one look at her — and the family members — and he wondered what he had barged in on.

A distinguished elderly gentleman came forward, nodded formally and remarked, "I apologize for my granddaughter, Mr. Hawkins. I am Montgomery Chan. Please, come in and allow us to make up for her lack of hospitality."

Hawk matched the man's formal bearing with his own. "Thank you, sir, but that is not necessary. It was not my intention to intrude on a private gathering. I simply misunderstood the Lieutenant's message. Good day, sir." He nodded to the others and left.

Hawk drove to Cholly's house, but if she was home, she did not answer the bell. He tried calling her on the phone and left several messages, none of which were returned. From her comments, it seemed there had been a showdown of some kind. And obviously, if her last remark was any indication, it had something to do with him.

Were they upset at his interest in her? Or hers in him? Not that she had declared her undying love for him, but at least he knew she was weakening, that she couldn't go on trying to ignore him, and how he felt about her, much longer.

If Hawk had gone down to the beach end of her street, he would have seen what looked like a forlorn bundle huddled up in a yellow slicker.

Cholly was perched on top of a large boulder, watching the storm-tossed waves pound at the rocks along the shore. The wind had picked up but she was oblivious to the elements. The only tempest that mattered now was her internal one.

Instead of feeling relief at having had a showdown with her family, Cholly was being bombarded with a kaleidoscope of emotions. She wasn't sorry about the results of the encounter. Cholly didn't buy into guilt trips. But she also wasn't happy about hurting the feelings of people who she knew cared about her.

The biggest problem had always been that she didn't conform to their idea of a well-behaved, dutiful daughter. No one ever believed her claims of trying; all they saw were her failures.

Many years ago, Cholly had come to a crossroads. She had to decide if she would live her life to conform to what they decreed was her destiny. Did she have the strength to insist she be allowed to live according to her concept of what was best for her? Cholly chose the latter path, and despite ongoing squabbles, never regretted her decision.

Until now. She still thought she had set the right priorities for herself, but what was she going to do about her feelings for Hawk?

Feelings! The one emotion Robo Cop didn't know how to handle.

# Chapter 45

A non-descript car pulled onto the end of the deserted pier. A man emerged and blended into the shadows on the side of the empty warehouses. The killer looked around cautiously, then walked slowly to the edge and held his knife out over the water. He tried to release it, but couldn't. "No, this was my grandfather's," he thought. A pause, then he returned it to his pocket and moved back toward the car.

---

The next morning Cholly sauntered into the office as if nothing had happened. She plopped a sack of donuts on the desk between them, muttered a "Good morning, Number Three," and walked over to get a cup of coffee.

Well, he sure didn't know what she was up to now, but he decided to play it safe and follow her lead. His only acknowledgement of her entrance was to help himself to a donut and go back to the file he was studying.

"Did that report come in from forensics yet?" Cholly bit into a glazed donut and perched on the end of her desk.

"Which one?" Hawk asked, eyeing her jogging suit.

"On the type of poison; you know, Sergeant, victim number three?" There was a sarcastic bite to her tone.

He ignored her attitude. He was getting good at that, and shuffled through several papers that were neatly stacked on his desk. "There's a prelim notation saying that it's a plant, probably oleander, but they won't put it in writing until they've finished the tests."

"God created the whole world in seven days; what's their problem?"

"What's yours?" he shot back.

"Nothing — everything. Damn!" She slapped the desk top to relieve her frustration. "Nothing is coming together. It's a long shot, but I'm going over to the Big Island and nose around. Winslow acted as if he was being straight with us, but my little itch tells me something isn't kosher with his story."

"When are we leaving?"

Cholly thought for a minute. "*We* aren't. You stay here and rag forensics —"

"That'll take all of ten minutes."

"Okay, Blue Eyes, the truth is you'll just be in the way." He raised that inquisitive eyebrow that she was growing to hate. "See what I'm wearing, Hawkins? I'm in disguise, undercover, etc., etc. Now how do you suppose I can disguise you, my jolly blonde giant?"

"Are we ever going to get past this haole thing, Lieutenant?"

"Only if you grow another head. Don't wait up for me, Mother, I may visit an old boyfriend when I'm done."

Cholly sailed out of the office with a satisfied smile on her face. She thought she'd handled that quite well. The only thing she didn't understand is why she threw in that bit about the old boyfriend. She didn't know any men on the Big Island.

---

At the Winslow Ranch, Cholly found the native manager. "So Kamuela wanted to deed some of their land over to the Ohana movement for Hawaiian homesteads, but Hiram wouldn't go along with his plan?" she repeated.

"We only talked about it briefly, but Mr. Hiram said no way was he going to go along with that idea," replied the manager. "He said maybe some day, but not now."

"How did Kamuela react to that?" Cholly asked.

"I don't know. He never came to the ranch office; he just went to the ranch house when there was a polo match here or if he threw a party," the manager responded.

"In general, how did the brothers get along?" asked Cholly.

"I never saw them together," he replied. "Course, there's always gossip about the old families."

"Like?"

"Mr. Hiram resented the money his brother spent on his horses, and I heard from one of the servants at the house that one day Kamuela got real hu'hu and shouted, 'If you can play Mah Jongg, I can have my horses.'"

"Is Hiram a big player?" asked Cholly.

"I've never heard if he was. Of course he doesn't spend a lot of social time here. Comes in, checks things out, leaves new orders, then goes back to Honolulu. Except around Christmas. He sometimes stays for a party or two then," he answered.

Suddenly, a photo on the wall caught Cholly's eye. It was the same photo she and Hawk had seen at Kamuela's home. Three people stood in the foreground: Kamuela and Hiram Winslow, and Miss Abigail Bingham. And in the background stood Keo MacGregor!

Three of the people in the photograph had been murdered. She needed to get back to Honolulu to warn Hiram before he was the next victim!

# Chapter 46

As Cholly rushed into Homicide, her desk phone began ringing. She answered breathlessly. After a brief conversation, she grabbed Hawk and raced into the Captain's office.

"Captain, I realized that three of the people in a photograph we found at Kamuela's house have been murdered. I raced back here so we could warn Hiram that he might be next, but Jimmy Lee just called to inform me that Hiram currently has a huge debt, thanks to his Mah Jongg losses. Perhaps we need to talk to him again."

Cap nodded. "Okay, kids, why don't you bring him back here for questioning. Do you want to take a couple of uniforms with you?"

Cholly and Hawk glanced at each other and shook their heads.

She answered, "I don't think it will be necessary. The two of us should be able to handle one middle-aged man."

Hawk glanced at Winslow's address and started toward the door. Cholly removed the gun from her purse and put it in a holster at her waist, grabbed a manila envelope from the desk and followed him out.

"Where's Maliki Drive?"

"Up on the mountain, overlooking the city. It's a very classy neighborhood."

"We get nothing but the best, right partner?"

Hawk took the switchback turns in stride, then pulled up in front of the large black wrought-iron gates guarding a stately old mansion. "This looks like something from the east coast, not Hawaii," he commented.

The grounds were well kept up, but the white-painted columns on the front porch appeared to be getting gray with age. The whole area had a feeling of elegant neglect.

After ringing the doorbell, they could hear the chimes echo throughout the house, but no one appeared. "Do you want me to check out back?" asked Hawk.

"I don't think it's really necessary. There's a sheer drop behind this property. There's nowhere to go, even if Winslow can climb over a six-foot-high iron fence with spikes on top.

The door finally opened and a shriveled-looking, old Filipino in a houseman's uniform greeted them suspiciously.

Showing her badge, Cholly asked for Winslow.

"Master no here. He go stable."

"Come on now, Mr. Winslow told us he never goes to the stables," responded Hawk impatiently.

The houseman shrugged. "He tell me he go take care of gol damn horses; they cost too gol damn much; he fix."

A look of horror crossed Cholly's face. "He's going to kill them!"

"I think he's gone over the edge now," Hawk agreed.

"We should call Mac Morales and warn him," said Cholly. Pushing past the houseman, they headed for Winslow's house phone.

"There's no answer," said Hawk. The two bolted for their cruiser.

---

As they pulled up to the stable buildings, they saw Hiram's car but heard no sounds. It was too quiet. Both pulled out their service revolvers.

"You take the back stalls and paddock. I'll start with the office, then the front building," Cholly said.

"Watch your back, kid," was Hawk's reply.

He moved cautiously around the outbuildings. Seeing nothing, he moved toward the pasture.

Cholly opened all the doors in the empty offices, then moved on to the tack room. Everything seemed in order so she entered the stall area.

Standing just inside the door, she listened carefully before inching her way down the row of stalls. She looked inside each one, then paused as a sound reached her ears. Moving more slowly, she suddenly stiffened as she realized she was smelling smoke.

Peering into the gloom at the back of the stable and looking for fire, Cholly turned at a sound behind her and found herself facing Hiram, who now stood between her and the door. He held a gas can and the wild look on his face told Cholly that she was dealing with a deranged man. He used the gasoline can he was holding to knock the gun out of her hand. It skittered across the room.

"It's over, Hiram. Put the can down and move away from it. You won't solve anything that way," she said evenly.

"There isn't anything left to solve, is there, Lieutenant? You and that pretty boy partner of yours, why couldn't you just leave it alone?" he snarled.

"You've killed four people. Didn't you think someone would mind?"

"Don't try your wit on me, girlie. And just for the record, I didn't mean to kill the first man. It was a mistake. In the torchlight he looked like Kamuela."

"Why didn't you just buy your brother's share of the business instead of killing him?" she demanded.

"I don't have any money left. It all went to my gambling. But even if I'd had the money, he would have never sold it to me. He was so damn hell-bent on just giving our land away to the Ohana." He added bitterly, "He never worked a day to earn any of it...."

Cholly's tone softened as she tried to stall. "I guess maybe I can see why you wanted to get rid of your brother, but did you have to kill two more innocent people to cover your tracks?" Where the hell was Hawk?

"Innocent, ha!" he exclaimed. "Abigail was a snob, always thought she was better than we were with her "Second Company" missionary family. And that MacGregor bastard — I saw some of his padded bills. My selfish brother was too stupid to even notice, but I did!"

As he spoke, Hiram began casually splashing more gasoline around the stalls and hallway. In his other hand he held a cigarette lighter. Hoping he was distracted by the movement, Cholly tried to inch closer. She heard the horses in the nearby stalls sense trouble and become agitated.

As though she still held her gun, she declared, "Okay, put the can down, *now*! And the lighter. Move away from them, *now*!"

Hiram glanced at her, laughed manically and thumbed the lighter. "It's too late. At least I'll have the pleasure of getting rid of his damn horses. Maybe, Lieutenant, if you can run fast enough, you can still save yourself."

He casually ignited a bale of hay next to a stall door and inched backward. The horses immediately panicked, kicking doors and screeching. As Cholly looked for an escape route, a stallion kicked down his stall door and headed for the open doorway.

The crazed horse headed straight for Hiram, who stood in the door. Throwing the can aside, Hiram turned and tried to outrun the terrified horse.

Cholly quickly noticed a rag and a bucket of water nearby. She wet the rag, covered her mouth, and began groping her way toward the front of the stables.

Seeing the billowing smoke from the pasture, Hawk ran to the stable building. As he struggled to free a hose mounted on the wall, Hiram came bolting out of the building. Hiram stopped, turned briefly to look behind him, then began running again. Just as he tripped and began to lose his balance, the stallion came racing out the same door and trampled Hiram.

Hawk began spraying water with the hose, but could see that the fire was too advanced, and there was no sign of Cholly. Dropping the hose, Hawk rushed into the burning building. He discovered an unconscious Cholly slumped not far from the door, the fire encircling her. As Hawk scooped her up, his shirt sleeve caught fire.

# Chapter 47

As the doctors and nurses worked on Cholly in the Emergency Room, the Captain kept an eye on Hawk, who could not take his eyes off Cholly. His clothes were smoke-stained, his face was sooty, and his right arm was bandaged.

"Relax, Hawk, the doctor says she's going to be okay," the Captain reassured him.

"But her face!" Hawk worried.

"It looks worse than it is. And even if there is a problem, they say a little plastic surgery will take care of it." He took Hawk by the uninjured arm. "Come on over here. You look exhausted. A cup of coffee might help."

Hawk resisted, still looking back at Cholly, but the Captain just kept tugging him along. "Really, she's fine. A few days and she'll be back to her old bitchy self."

Wincing as he moved his arm, Hawk replied, "We wouldn't want her any other way, would we?"

Looking past Hawk, the Captain smiled at Cholly. He gave Hawk a cup of coffee, took one for himself, and settled the two of them on a couch. After a few sips, he suddenly remembered what was in his pocket. Pulling a pink phone slip out, he handed it to Hawk. "With everything that's been going on, I forgot all about this. The call came in a few hours ago."

Hawk grabbed the note. Reading it, his shoulders sagged. Then he re-read it, as if not believing what it said. Then he looked back at Cholly.

---

A thin light shining down on the head of the bed was the only illumination in Cholly's hospital room. Cholly was finally asleep. The door opened and a shadowy figure moved noiselessly over to stand by the bed, looking down at her.

As if sensing his presence, Cholly tried to open her eyes and focus on the figure. "Hawk?" she asked fuzzily.

"I'm here." He reached out and covered her hand with his.

"Are you all right?" she asked.

"Just a few blisters, nothing serious," he replied softly.

She sighed. She felt at a loss for words and winced as she tried to shift her weight.

"What happened to Winslow?" she finally managed.

"The horses panicked. One of the stallions ran him down."

Trying to be flip, Cholly said, "That'll save us a couple days in court."

Expecting to hear a flip reply from Hawk, Cholly was troubled when he remained silent.

Hesitatingly, she continued. "I've kind of been out of it the last couple of days, but I overheard the nurses talking. They said you saved my life."

"Just doin' my job, ma'am," he drawled.

"Uh hm. So what's the score now, officer?"

"Well, counting Rose's Bar …."

"We don't count Rose's."

"Well, I do, so that makes it two to one." He paused. "I guess that means I still own you, huh?"

"What are you going to do about it?" she asked flirtatiously.

Softly, Hawk replied, "Not much, I'm afraid."

As he shifted, Cholly could see that he was dressed in a navy-colored pea jacket. "Hawk, what's going on?"

"I'm leaving. My ship sails in an hour."

Cholly had been hazy from the pain medication, but suddenly found herself quite alert, and part of a world that was falling apart. She was stricken.

"Leaving … but what … about your job … us?"

Hawk's anguish was evident as he answered her. "There can't be any us … at least not now, and maybe never."

"I don't understand, Hawk. What's happened?"

Instead of answering her, he just squeezed her hand.

"Were you going to leave without an explanation?" she asked hotly.

Wearily, he replied, "I can't tell ...."

Cholly exploded at him. "You come in ... wreck my lifestyle ... then give me this crap. I'm a cop for God's sake!"

She suddenly realized that he was dressed in seaman's garb.

"I guess I owe you that much. I really did want to stay here, try and start a new life, but then ...." His voice broke, causing him to pause.

"What's happened?"

"Jian Wa is dead. They claim he was killed by 'friendly fire.'"

"What in the hell are you talking about?"

"Operation Yellowbird Trail."

Cholly felt confused. "The businessmen trying to smuggle dissidents out before China takes over Hong Kong?"

"Yes, he was one of the founders," answered Hawk.

"And the smugglers, especially the Triad, are working to help out, right?"

"Yeah, and what a great cover that would be to help them get rid of their enemies," Hawk retorted bitterly.

"Are you sure?"

"That's what I'm going out there to find out."

"If you survive that mission, then what?" Cholly asked fearfully.

"I'll have to take his place."

Cholly turned her head away to hide the tears that were already spilling over. Biting her lip, she tried to regain her composure.

"And you don't even speak Chinese," she smarted off.

Hawk responded in Mandarin, "I'll get by."

Cholly was shocked to hear his native accent.

Trying to sound light-hearted, Hawk continued. "I still owe you one for that meal at the Black Hole. And all the names you called me, but I guess I'll have to wait until you're back in fighting shape."

She tightened her hold on his hand and looked closely at his face. "I heal fast," she answered.

Then her eyes widened as she finally got a good look at him. His hair had been dyed black, he was growing a beard, and he wore a seaman's knit cap.

"Maybe some day, kid … if you see a scruffy old sailor and he speaks to you in Mandarin … be nice to him. He might be someone you once loved." Hawk slipped his hand out of hers and headed toward the door. "I love you," he said in Mandarin as he opened the door.

Dazed by what was happening, it took a moment for Cholly to realize he was leaving. "I love you, too," she yelled at his back. "And don't you dare go and get yourself killed, Number Three. I'm not finished with you yet!"

# Chapter 48

Cholly's recovery was right on schedule; she was discharged from the hospital in a few days and sent home to finish healing. Her health was improving, but not her spirits. Kam, finally mobile, came often to check on her and help her.

Two weeks later, her favorite Tutu rang the doorbell. Kam opened the door to a woman laden with flowers and a lauhala basket.

He kissed her in welcome. "Aloha, Aunty, I'm so glad you're back."

"I came as soon as I could leave Uncle Joe. How is she?"

Kam lowered his voice. "Physically she's doing okay, but she just sits and stares out at the ocean all day long. I think she needs you."

Tutu walked out to the lanai where Cholly was curled up in an oversized Papa-san chair, staring at the water. Cholly didn't notice her until she was standing right in front of her.

"Oh, Tutu, I'm so glad you're back!" She threw herself into her grandmother's arms.

"I'm so sorry I couldn't get back sooner," Tutu said with concern as she looked at her granddaughter's face.

"The main thing is you're here now!"

Tutu continued to scrutinize Cholly, not just her face, but as if she were looking for something deeper. "So, your face will be all right, but what about the rest of you?"

Cholly replied in a flat, listless tone of voice, "I'm fine." She looked almost slovenly.

"Well, you could have fooled me," was Tutu's reply. "From what I was told, all you've been doing is sitting around feeling sorry for yourself and staring at a path to China."

Cholly reacted angrily, "That's not true!"

"Then why haven't you gone back to work?"

"I ... I ... tried ... but ...."

"Why won't you see the police psychiatrist?"

"It won't help."

"How do you know? Almost losing your life is a hard thing to deal with!"

"Oh, Tutu, it's not the fire. It's ... life. I ... I don't care if I ever go back to work. I don't care about anything."

"I think maybe you care too much," Tutu replied.

Cholly gave her a puzzled look.

"Hawk's leaving you ... the fact you discovered there's more to life than being Super Cop."

Cholly began pacing restlessly. Then she said thoughtfully, "I remember reading that when conquerors take over a people, they need to give them something of

221

value to believe in, to replace what they've lost. I guess that's what I need. My old lifestyle doesn't work anymore … but I don't know what to do … where to turn."

Tutu tisked. "Solutions don't have to be complicated, Kaloke. You can't bring Hawk back, so accept it and get on with your life. And if you don't like the old one, find something new to take its place."

# Chapter 49

Taking her grandmother's advice to heart, Cholly booked herself on a cruise to Asia and just two weeks later, Kam walked her to the cruise ship terminal. "I could see you traipsing to a monastery or something, but Tillie the tourist?"

"I've never been just one of the crowd. Maybe I can lose myself in the flow."

They hugged goodbye and Cholly gave him a "thumbs up" sign as she walked away. She turned and tried to impersonate the movie star: "I'll be back, baby."

---

And exactly three months later, Cholly finally returned from her travels and went back to work. On her first day, the department threw her a welcome back party. As everyone was leaving, Cholly went into the Captain's office and plopped down in his chair.

With a bit more reserve than usual, the Captain asked, "So, how does it feel to be home?"

"Same old, same old."

"Do you want to warm a desk for a while or get back on the street?"

"What do you think?" she answered brashly, then took a closer look at him. "Okay, Cap, what's up?"

"What are you talking about?" he asked innocently.

"I know you too well. When something's bothering you, your left eye twitches."

"Does not." He blinked both eyes. "See?"

She just glared at him silently as he fidgeted.

Finally, quietly, he stammered out, "I … I … think … I have some bad news. I can't confirm anything …"

There was still no response from her.

Finally, he blurted out, "The Asian grapevine says Hawk's disappeared. They … they think he's dead."

Cholly looked inward. "No, I don't think so. I … I … I'd know if something had happened to him."

The Captain replied, "I hope you're right."

# Chapter 50

Cholly threw herself into her police work and tried to keep her mind off Hawk. It wasn't easy. As days became weeks and weeks became months, Cholly had a daily fight concentrating on her job.

And no one was more aware of this than Kam. More and more frequently he found himself covering for her. "Damn it, Cholly, what the hell was the matter with you this morning? Letting the perp get the drop on you — hell I wouldn't have believed it if I hadn't seen it with my own eyes. You keep this up and you're gonna get us both killed one of these days!"

Cholly felt the tears welling in her eyes. She didn't even try to defend herself; she knew Kam was right. With her head down, she made her way to the restroom. She didn't want anyone to see her cry. Tears were once a stranger to Cholly, but now they seemed to be an almost daily occurrence.

Kam was right; each day Cholly found it more difficult to stay focused. Police work depended on a sharp mind and she couldn't afford to put anyone in danger, especially Kam. She vowed, for the umpteenth time, to get her act together.

But her concentration did not improve. The finale to this drama was literally the last straw. Cholly and Kam had an arrest warrant for a suspect whom they knew to be on the island. There were two places where he could probably be found.

Kam chose the north shore location, while Cholly would work the area near Pearl Harbor, where the suspect was known to have connections.

She covertly checked out a number of places where he was known to hang out, found him, arrested him and took him to police headquarters. But there, as the saying goes, things went south pretty quickly — she had arrested his twin brother!

---

A few days later, as Cholly came into the department, one of the officers addressed her with a very strained look on his face. "Cholly, the Police Commissioner is in the Captain's office and they want to see you immediately."

She was smart enough to know that she was being called on the carpet due to the arrest mistake she had made. But she was not prepared for her reception. The look on her uncle's face was enough to tell her she was in serious trouble.

The commissioner didn't mince any words. "For years I've been aware that I was blessed with the sharpest female officer in the whole state. Some of your accomplishments have become so legendary that they outshine many of the male officers' efforts. But now the shit has hit the fan — big time."

The Cholly who was known to have the fastest mouth in the place bit her lip. She didn't begin to know what to say. She looked at the Captain, but he just shook his head.

The Commissioner continued, "We've been discussing the situation and I've decided to put you back 'on probation.' You screw up one more time and I'll probaby have to fire you."

He looked at the Captain and said, "I'm sorry, I know she's been one of your best officers as well as your niece, but these last few months she's become a wild card, and not in a good way. The Department can't take that kind of heat."

As soon as she was dismissed, Cholly raced to the restroom, tears welling in her eyes once more. "When am I going to be able to get my act together?" she wondered.

---

The answer came only two weeks later. As she was going over some paperwork, the phone on her desk rang.

"Homicide, Lt. Chan," she said as she answered the call.

"This is Quantas Airlines, Lieutenant. We are bringing a special delivery for you on Flight 890. You will need to pick it up at the passenger terminal."

This was puzzling. "What time?"

"Two twenty."

---

Cholly waited at the arrival gate. It appeared that all of the passengers had deplaned and she was just trying to find someone to ask about her delivery when a flight attendant walked out with a half Asian boy of about seven. He was holding a photograph of Cholly in his hand.

"Are you Lieutenant Chan?" asked the flight attendant. "I'll need to see a photo ID."

A stunned Cholly pulled out her police ID. After the attendant said thank you, she began to walk away with the rest of the flight crew.

"Wait! What's this about?"

"All I know is I was supposed to hand him over to you. I don't know any more, but his papers are supposed to be in his backpack."

At a loss for words, Cholly finally managed to ask in Mandarin, "What's your name?"

The boy replied, "I speak English. My name is Alex." He turned around and added, "There's a letter for you in my backpack."

In great confusion, Cholly pulled out the letter. Before she could look at it, Alex grabbed her hand. Please, Miss Cholly, I'm very thirsty. May I get a drink of water?"

She hesitated a moment, then took his hand and headed over to a snack area. She got him a cold drink and a cookie, then sat with him to finally read the letter.

It was from Hawk. She read, "Alex is the son of my friend Yiang. I adopted him after his father's death. I've kept him hidden in a rural village, but I can no longer protect him there. You are the only one I can trust to keep him safe. Alex will tell you all you need to know. If my luck holds out, I'll be there soon. If I don't make it, remember my last words to you."

Cholly sat down in stunned silence.

Alex took her hand and said, "I am going to live with you. I am seven years old and my name is Alexander

Woodrow Hawkins the fourth. Most people call me Alex, but my daddy says you can call me Number Four."

A shocked Cholly held Alex's hand while he chattered away. Suddenly he stopped and fought back tears. "Miss Cholly, do you think my daddy will be here soon? Uncle Lee says some bad men want to hurt him ... us ...."

Although a bit unsure of herself, Cholly dropped down on one knee in front of Alex. Looking eye to eye, she paused only a moment, then put her arms around him.

"Honey, your daddy is a very smart, and very brave man. If he says he'll be here, he'll make it."

She stood up, took his hand again and gave him a big smile. "And now, Number Four, let's go home."

# Chapter 51

The Cholly-Alex honeymoon was short-lived. She planned to stay home with Alex for a few days, but when she contemplated going back to work, she realized that her unpredictable schedule made parenting alone very difficult. Finding a good school was not the problem. Since he spoke English, he could go to any Island school, and she liked the idea of sending him to her alma mater, Punahou School. But that didn't solve the problem of where he could go between the end of his school day and the end of her often-unpredictable work day.

She struggled with the logic of hiring a live-in housekeeper. It just wasn't an option she was thrilled with. Luckily, fate stepped in when she stopped by headquarters during lunch. As she mentioned her predicament — well, actually whined about it to her department buddies — one of them remarked that he might have an answer. His neighbor's sister had left her job on the mainland, moved back to the Islands and was living with the neighbors. Marge was former teacher, and he'd heard that she wanted work that was part time.

Cholly arranged their meeting after Alex had gone to bed. Despite the fact that she had grown up with a household full of servants, she had no idea of how to go about hiring someone for a job that might be considered flexible, even different. She really didn't even know what to call it. And she had no intention of asking for advice from her sisters-in-law or any other family members.

"Motor-mouth," as Kam liked to call her, was almost tongue tied as she realized she didn't know how to start the interview, or even what to ask. Marge had spent 25 years dealing with all kinds of situations with parents. It was easy for her to realize that Cholly had no idea of what she needed, except help with a capital "H."

"Lieutenant, I've heard what a great cop you are, but it's obvious you are in foreign territory when it comes to kids, so let's just keep it simple and tell me what you need and we'll work it out."

Her approach was so straight-forward and kind. Cholly didn't realize she had been holding her breath until she let it out in one big whoosh. "I *do* need help, but I don't know what kind or how to get it."

Marge let out a hearty laugh and asked, "In that case, Lieutenant, may I question you?"

Cholly relaxed a bit and nodded.

"For starters, do you need someone full time, maybe even live-in, that type of help?"

"No, I don't think so. Hopefully I can take him to school every morning, but after-school hours and those occasions when I might have night calls are my problem. I think."

"So what you need, Lieutenant, is what some folks call "flex" help."

"First, Marge, please call me Cholly, and second, yes, that would be a perfect name for this job. I want to do as much as I can to be a mother to him, but my job is so very unpredictable...." Her voice trailed off, and to her surprise, she realized she was fighting back tears.

Marge moved closer and laid a hand over Cholly's. "Honey, for decades I've seen single mothers trying to build what I call an "alone" life for their families. We live

231

less than 15 minutes away, so it would be no problem for me to stay late sometime, or if you had a call in the middle of the night, I could come out and stay with him."

For the first time in months, Cholly felt as if she was getting her life into some kind of order.

# Chapter 52

It was a week before Christmas and Cholly could hardly believe how much her life had changed in the last year. She looked a little older, her hair was a little shorter, and sometimes she was told that her flat replies made it sound like she wasn't interested in some people's conversations, but life at home was surprisingly happy.

She was seated at her desk, going over some reports. The Captain walked in and glanced at his wristwatch. "Why don't you call it a day so you and Alex won't have to rush to get out to the luau?"

Closing the folder she'd been working on, Cholly pushed back her chair and gave a half-whispered answer. "Thanks, Cap, but I think we'll skip it — I'm kind of tired."

The Captain sat on the corner of her desk. "Look, Cholly, I know holiday time can be a downer, but you know how much Alex likes to be with the kids. If you want to stay just for dinner, I'll bring him home later. He's ohana now and feels right at home even when you aren't there."

It took considerable effort for her to get herself out of her chair, a fact the Captain noticed. "You feeling okay? There's a lot of flu going around…."

"No, I'm fine, I — I just …."

The Captain put his arm around her. "Cholly, I know how hard it is for you. You are worn out with waiting, hoping …."

She pulled away and replied in a stronger tone, "Look, I'm okay. I just have to do it my way, to survive the best way that works for me. But I don't want Alex to lose out because of that. I'll bring him over, maybe stay for a while and then you can bring him home."

Despite the happy atmosphere at the luau, Cholly stayed only until the food was ready, then took some home to eat. She just couldn't deal with small talk and the inevitable questions. She felt like having a card made up that read, "No, we haven't heard from him."

Eating on the lanai, she stared out across the water toward China — a habit that hadn't changed since she returned to Honolulu. She tried not to let anyone see her cry, but even Alex sometimes made a comment about it. When he did, she simply told him she'd had a rough day at work and he accepted that fact. But there were some nights when she found him crying after he'd gone to bed. And on those nights, they simply wrapped their arms around each other — they didn't need to say a word.

As she looked at the water, she began thinking about Alex's upcoming birthday. When she had asked him how he wanted to celebrate it, he had surprised her by asking if they could go over to Maui and stay at the hotel on the mountaintop so he could see snow for the first time.

She was happy to say yes, for it held no memories for her. But Alex caught her off guard when he asked if he could learn to ski while they were there. Cholly had never had any desire to ski, so they both had to sign up for lessons and buy the right clothing for their adventure. She had actually felt light-hearted as they tried on clothes and he told her that one of his classmates had recommended buying a thick pair of pants so it wouldn't hurt when he fell down.

Christmas would be only three days after their ski trip, so she decided to see if they could stay there over the holiday, too. It was getting harder and harder for her to go to happy affairs and try to keep a smile on her face. She just wanted to be alone with her pain, but she couldn't deny Alex the chance to have a good time with the cousins and friends.

At work the next day, the Captain had a very serious look on his face when she came into the office after a stake out. He motioned her to sit down and the look on his face told her this wasn't going to be a light-hearted conversation.

"After you left and the kikis were playing in the next room, the women ganged up on me," he complained.

"What in the hell are you talking about?"

"They are all worried about you. Truly, we all are, but they started listing things I hadn't noticed."

"Like what?" she asked in a cold tone. She just wasn't in the mood for another lecture.

He sat down at his desk and put his head in his hands, either stalling for time or trying to figure out how to talk to her.

"You've lost weight, you look like hell, and your work is starting to suffer again —"

She cut him off. "Like hell it has. I may do things a little differently — I sure can't hot dog around like I used to because of Alex —"

"Cholly, chill. No one knows better than I do how hard you work to keep up, and you couldn't do a better job with Alex if you were his birth mother. But the truth is, Cholly, it *is* starting to take its toll on you."

235

Cholly collapsed into her chair. "In what way?" It was almost a whisper, as if she didn't have the energy to fight any more.

He sat down, fidgeting with the papers on his desk. Finally, softly, he said, "I think the time has come when," he could hardly speak, "when you — we — maybe need to accept that Hawk can't make it out, that maybe he's dead."

# Chapter 53

Cholly was seated strapping on her skis when she felt a tug on her jacket and Alex started to laugh.

"Don't you dare try to put that snowball down my neck, you little devil—" She stifled her laugh as she spun around to push him away.

"Kam says he does that to his sister all the time and I should try it."

"Not if you want to be able to sit down comfortably for the rest of the week."

"Aw, Cholly, you know you've never spanked me."

She laughed and gave him a playful poke on his shoulder. "There's always a first time, kiddo."

"You know you would never hurt me."

She leaned over and gave him a hug. "I love you so much."

Unwittingly, her eyes teared up, and as she was blinking them away, she caught her breath. For a second, she thought she saw a man who looked like Hawk. She wiped her eyes for a better look, but he had pushed off and was on his way down the mountain.

"What's the matter, Cholly? You look funny but not in a laughing way."

It took her a moment to clear her throat enough to reply. "I thought I saw a friend from college, but I guess I was wrong."

That night when she was tucking him into bed, he caught her off guard with a question. "Aren't we going home to spend Christmas with the family?"

"Well, I thought since we were having so much fun here...."

"Yeah, but I want to be with the other kids to open our presents."

Of course she acquiesced, and they went back to Honolulu on Christmas Eve. When they got back, she called the Captain and said she wasn't feeling well, and asked if he would pick Alex up and let him stay at his house. It was a lie, but she just couldn't deal with trying to carry on as usual.

On Christmas morning, Alex called and woke her up to wish her a merry Christmas. He asked if she would be there for dinner. She continued her lie by saying she wasn't feeling well, but she knew the Captain would bring him back home the following day.

Cholly tried to go back to sleep, but finally gave up, brewed some coffee and took it out on the lanai to drink. The breeze shifted and there was a small tinkling sound coming from the small bells strung about the garden.

Her maudlin thoughts followed their usual path: It would have been a perfect day if ....

For once, she became annoyed with herself. "Okay, sister, you have got to get hold of yourself. This isn't good for you and it certainly isn't good for the boy. You're not the first woman who has lost her man in a war. You owe it to him to give Alex a happy home, not one drowning in sorrow."

Her hand was trembling so much, she spilled some coffee on the pillow next to her. She picked it up and viciously threw it across the lanai.

Pent-up tears started to flow and she just couldn't stop crying. She heard the phone ring, but let the answering machine pick up the call.

Finally, exhausted by her emotions, Cholly actually dozed off. She had slept very little during the night, and now her deep sleep kept getting interrupted by dreams that would only add to her distress when she woke up.

She didn't know how many hours she had been sleeping, but eventually the ringing of the door bell woke her. She wasn't expecting anyone and her eyes were so puffy from crying that she could hardly see, so she chose to ignore it. There was no one she wanted to see.

A few minutes later she heard a ship's horn blasting away from across the water that lapped at her shore. Stiff from sleeping in a chair, she got up and walked across to face the water. The ship was an inter-island steamer returning from carrying tourists out for a day on the water. She could hear the music from the Lido Deck and see folks waving to the people left at the beach near her.

Still groggy from her tear-induced sleep, Cholly felt a strange sensation. Was she still half asleep? But then she felt the hair on the back of her neck stiffen and she knew she was not alone. She felt a presence at her back and when a strong arm encircled her waist, she had to take a deep breath before letting out, "How did you get in?"

The response was a soft kiss that brushed the side of her neck and then a chuckle, "You forgot, I never met a lock I couldn't open."

239

As she spun around in his arms, she hardly recognized him. Hawk was thin, scarred, and looked exhausted.

She didn't know what to say, so blurted out, "Why didn't you let us know —"

"I didn't have time. I stowed away on a cargo ship…"

He couldn't finish, because Cholly had pulled his head down and was giving him a kiss that she hoped would never end.

Finally, they paused. She looked at him closely and said, "You look like death warmed over."

Leaning on her heavily, he managed a smirk and said, "I'm saving all my strength for the bedroom."

But as she led him to the bedroom, he could barely lift his feet, and the moment he had shuffled into the room, he collapsed onto the bed. Cholly turned to disconnect the phone on the nightstand, and when she turned back to him seconds later, he was sound asleep.

Cholly spent a restless night. She tried to sleep, but having Hawk so near kept her nerves jangling. Hawk didn't seem to even know she was there. His deep sleep was like that of the dead. By mid-morning, after he had been asleep all evening and night, Hawk began to move about, but seemed unable to awaken. Cholly, who had watched over him for hours, was struck by how gaunt and unhealthy he looked. She suddenly realized that he needed immediate medical attention. Cholly knew it was time to call the rescue squad.

# Chapter 54

As Cholly sat by the still-unconscious Hawk's bed, the doctor returned to the hospital room to check on him. "I expect that he will be waking up soon," he told her. "He was very dehydrated and the intravenous infusions we have been giving him will make a big difference. That was the major problem we needed to treat. Is there anything I can do for you? I don't want to offend you, but you look like hell."

Cholly shook her head with a smile, and returned her gaze to Hawk as the doctor left the room. She noticed him beginning to stir and felt herself relaxing for the first time in hours.

She laid her head against the back of the chair and closed her eyes for just a few minutes.

Two hours later, the door opened slowly and the Captain peeked in to find Cholly fast asleep in the chair by the bed, next to an almost fully-awake Hawk. He stepped into the room with a firm grip on the wrist of Alex, who was beside himself with excitement. The stern instructions the Captain had given to Alex on the way to the hospital were quickly forgotten as the boy tore himself free and launched himself onto the bed.

The motion and noise awoke Cholly with a start, and tears sprang to her eyes as she watched Hawk wrap his arms around "their" son. Without thinking, she propelled herself onto the Alex-Hawk pile to hug them both, laughing and crying at the same time.

Hawk and Alex laughed too, but Hawk's eyes became serious when he met Cholly's gaze. His throat was dry and his voice hoarse as he whispered, "I've been to hell, but it was the thought of you and Alex that helped me make my way back."

A little embarrassed that he was witnessing an intimate scene, the Captain cleared his throat and proceeded to take command. "In my humble opinion, it's time you two stopped playing games and admitted how much you love each other. I am a patient man, but I've had enough and am taking matters into my own hands." He turned to the doorway. "You can come in now," he called.

In walked Cholly's other Uncle Kimo, a respected Honolulu judge.

The Captain continued, "Hawk, you're too sick right now to take part in a traditional wedding ceremony, so I've arranged for an informal ceremony here and now! We're all tired of you two pussy-footing around. Later on, when you've regained your strength, we'll have the traditional ceremony and a party just like the luau you attended when Pualani got married."

A broad smile crept across Hawk's face. He looked up at Cholly and said, "And do you promise it will have the same ending?"

Cholly choked back a laugh and nodded. Before she could respond, Hawk said, "Well in that case, I DO!"

## *The End*

www.ingramcontent.com/pod-product-compliance
Lightning Source LLC
Chambersburg PA
CBHW050511260626
47157CB00004B/1275

*  9  7  8  0  9  9  6  6  7  4  0  3  4  *